The Starlight Commune

Andrew Benzie Books
Martinez, California

Published by Andrew Benzie Books
www.andrewbenziebooks.com

Printed in the United States of America.

First Edition: August 2023

10 9 8 7 6 5 4 3 2 1

ISBN 978-1-950562-53-4

Cover and book design by Andrew Benzie

A dream of the world as it could have been…
and will become.

CONTENTS

CHAPTER ONE

THE GATHERING

Professor João da Gama sat in his office in the history department at the University of Hawaii, Mãnoa campus. It was the end of his day, the end of office hours. No more students today asking questions, or worse, arguing about their grades on their final term paper. It was also his last day after a 30-year career teaching not only in the history department but also in the geography department. *A distinguished career*, he reminded himself. *But I'm not going to talk myself out of retiring. I deserve some down time, but more importantly time to work on a personal project with my friends.*

João hadn't quite worked out all the details of the project that had taken root in his mind a month ago. Something to do with the history of the Horn of Africa, the horn-shaped land formation that forms the easternmost point of the African continent, projecting into the Indian Ocean south of the Arabian Peninsula. He and several of his colleagues in the history, anthropology and political science departments had long studied and written about East Africa in the 15th and 16th centuries. Looking back on his career he was amazed at how well he and those colleagues—Sandra Bevilacqua, Yuen Ho Wan, Abbas Amir, Horacio Fuente and Makelle Ringhiera—had worked together. Over the past few months, they had been discussing doing some joint research into that region during that era, in particular the Horn of Africa. The only problem was the logistics of getting together or working separately; they all lived in different parts of Oahu, but had fantasized spending a month or two together somewhere, like a retreat where they could devote themselves full time and without distraction to their dream project.

João had also been studying marine navigation during the 15th century, especially navigation using the so-called "spherical astrolabe." That device had been continually improved since Arab navigators began using them in the 10th century. The Portuguese mariners used them to great advantage in their maritime explorations. For at least the past 10 years João had been collecting different versions of the device, gradually hunting specifically for the more advanced ones. He was hoping to fold his obsession with the devices into his as yet undeveloped idea for a research project into 15th century Horn of Africa.

But João's immediate project was to purchase a home. A bigger home than the one he and his late wife had owned for the past 25 years. It wasn't just the size of his home that motivated him to move. There were just too many memories, especially the memory of his wife's long illness leading to her death. Plus, his twin sons had left the nest and were attending college at UCLA. He was hoping to move away from Oahu and find something in a more rural environment, such as the island of Molokai. He had a real estate agent, Margaret Kahale, working for him, scouring the island.

When João arrived home from the university he checked his messages. There was one from Margaret, who sounded excited. She was suggesting he might want to take a look at a long-deserted mansion on Molokai. He listened to her message again: "João, Margaret. You won't believe what I found—a 19th century mansion, unoccupied for the past couple of years. It's on Molokai. I definitely think you should check it out. I suggest we fly to Molokai from Honolulu. From the airport we'll head north on Highway 460, then onto Highway 470. We pass Kualapu'u and continue on Highway 470 to Kalaupapa. I'm sure you've heard of that tongue of land extending into the Pacific below the sea cliffs; maybe you've been there. That little peninsula is where I found this ancient mansion that practically backs up to parkland—no nosy neighbors! It dates back to the 1870s. Some eccentric old gentleman owns it. His agent tells me it's mostly empty, but not dilapidated. I think you should check it out."

João called Margaret back and agreed to meet her at the airport and fly there. He was excited and looking forward to seeing the property.

CHAPTER TWO

THE DISCOVERY

"I thought you said it wasn't dilapidated." João and Margaret were sitting at a card table in the parlor and examining the ancient, yellowed floor plan for all three floors and the basement.

"I'm sorry, João. My counterpart described it as problem free. But really, other than the leak in the roof and several broken windows, I don't see anything that couldn't be dealt with cheaply. And it recently passed a structural examination by an architectural firm."

João looked skeptical. "I don't know. The plans show six attics, two at each end of the building, one above the room labeled `staff quarters,' and one directly above the master bedroom. I wouldn't be surprised if the roof was leaking into one of them, maybe all of them." Rolling up the plans he said, "Let's walk around the grounds before I make up my mind. I have to say, the property is beautiful. And to be honest, I think even if the place needs a new roof, it's definitely worth the asking price."

The two of them walked out the front door and around the side of the house to the back. The grounds there rose gently for about 50 yards, terminating at a little hilltop with a stunning view of the rest of the Kalaupapa peninsula, most of which had been converted to parkland. They sat on two three-foot-high flat stones that were part of a U-shaped group of similar stones that seemed to have been placed there long ago to take advantage of the view. "You know, Margaret, this view alone might convince me to take the place. What do you know about the owner?"

"I learned a little about the guy from the listing agent. The owner's name is Mon Lao. He's the great grandson of a Chinese diplomat who had been posted all over the world. The diplomat retired in Hawaii in 1904 and had this place built. The retired diplomat lived here for something like 20 years before he died. After that each of his descendants inherited the property. But none of them wanted to live here and eventually Mon Lao inherited it. He lived here for a year, then moved out, and put the place up for sale a month ago. There has been some interest in the place, but things move slowly in Hawaii, especially on Molokai. But that said, if I were you, I'd make up my mind sooner rather than later, especially at this price."

João didn't waste time trying to decide. He loved the building, the grounds and the location on the island of Molokai. *What's not to like? Only the roof leak.* But he decided to go for it. He made an offer, which was accepted within 24 hours. The speed of acceptance worried him a little, made him suspicious that there were more problems with the place.

After he completed the sale, he was relieved to find that the roof leak wasn't as bad as he had feared. After having it repaired João busied himself with replacing the two broken windows and having the entire house cleaned from top to bottom. He decided to hire a landscape gardener and an assistant to help him figure out what to do with the overgrown front and back yards. He hired specialists to clean out and repair the fireplaces and chimneys. He had the carpeting ripped up and the magnificent hardwood floors refinished. He replaced the very dated and ugly kitchen appliances in the main floor kitchen. He hired a full-time cook from the nearby village. The staff kitchen in the basement he decided to leave be. The stove was in decent shape. Next to it was a huge oven for baking bread in the old-fashioned way.

Finally, he was ready to take a look at the attics.

The two at the ends of the building were empty, as was the attic above the staff quarters. But inside the one above the master bedroom were a couple of cardboard boxes, some antique furniture, and a very large wood-and-brass steamer trunk. Although he was only looking into the attic from the top of the ladder, he could see that the trunk was not only beautiful but it would be a bitch to remove.

Nevertheless, he decided he wouldn't be able to sleep until he had a look at that trunk. His two gardeners figured out a way to rig up a web of rope on the floor of the attic and lift the trunk onto the rope web. Then they carefully lowered the harnessed trunk through the trap door to the floor of the bedroom. João was relieved that the guys hadn't injured themselves or damaged the trunk.

He couldn't wait to have a look inside. The trunk had a leather strap around it at each end. The ends of each strap fit into a brass padlock. There didn't seem to be a key for the locks, but it hardly mattered since the leather straps were rotten in places. João easily broke and removed each strap, took a breath, and gingerly opened the hinged lid of the trunk.

At first João was disappointed. The trunk appeared to be full of books. Not even particularly valuable or rare books from the looks of them. He removed the books and set them on his bedroom work table. With the books out of the way, he could see a worn leather briefcase and a wood-and-brass chest. The chest was square and looked to be about two feet on a side. João lifted both the briefcase and chest out and set them on the coffee table.

He opened the briefcase first. Inside he saw a strange-looking book and two separate packets of papers. He took them out and set them aside for the moment. João opened the little wood-and-brass chest and removed an object wrapped in what looked like a Turkish kilim rug. He walked back to the coffee table and set the object down. He carefully unwrapped the kilim. Inside was an ancient maritime navigational tool called a spherical astrolabe. It was mounted on a small pedestal; probably the strangest spherical astrolabe he had ever encountered or seen in history books or estate-sale catalogs.

João turned his attention to the papers. One packet appeared to be written in Chinese, which João couldn't read. The second packet was written in Somaliña, which João could read.

But the book was the most exotic item in the trunk. João carried it to the couch and sat down. The book was bound in black leather. Embossed on the cover were two words, one on top of the other, in two languages he was familiar with. The word ግራኝ embossed on top was the word "Grañ" written in Amharic. The word عراني below it was "Grañ" written in Arabic. He knew the word. It was the nickname of the infamous Somali warlord who almost conquered Abyssinia in the 16th century. Inside the leather covers there appeared to be about 70 pages of an ancient type of rag paper. They were sewn together in groups of ten pages using linen thread in a chain stitch. The front and back pages were glued to linen-covered heavy rag paper. The black leather binding was glued to that.

João was astonished when he read the title page: "<u>From the Future to the Past, by Dr. Horacio Fuente, Mogadishu, Somalia. 1455.</u>" João gasped, then chuckled. *I can't wait to see the expression on Horacio's face when I show him this!* Then he realized the date was about 100 years *before* the rise of Grañ. He assumed someone must have added the word "Grañ" to the leather cover later.

João turned the pages slowly, marveling at the clear handwritten text. João was surprised that it was written in modern English, given that the date on the title page was 1455. But what surprised him even more than the date, more than the language, and more than the book's appearance, was the chapter in which the author provided a detailed drawing of a spherical astrolabe:

On the following pages there were instructions for converting the astrolabe into what the author called a time machine. João sat back and let what he was reading sink in. Accompanying the instructions and the drawing was this statement from the author:

The strangest thing about having found myself in Mogadishu was that it seemed to be a different Mogadishu than the one described in history books. Be that as it may, soon I no longer wanted to return to my former time. This version of Mogadishu is now my home. My beautiful astrolabe, had I not fallen and broken something inside it, might have made another journey to another time. But even if it could be repaired, I will not go with it. My daughter Alessandra will send it off to whatever destiny awaits it. I was fortunate that Alessandra could ensure a pre-ordained future for my spherical astrolabe. When I told her what my history books had said about the date that the fleet of Vasco da Gama would anchor offshore Mogadishu, we formulated a plan wherein she would hire a fishing boat to take her there and present the astrolabe to the Captain. I will remain here, rooted in the past, married to a wonderful woman, father of a wonderful daughter, and together we'll make a beautiful future.

Unable to take his mind away from what he had just read, João got up and went to the kitchen to make himself a cup of tea. He took his tea back to the couch and resumed reading the book. He couldn't make heads nor tails of the detailed description of how the astrolabe had been converted into a time machine. *Or a would-be time machine? Could this be an elaborate joke?*

But the instructions themselves were fairly clear and detailed, even if they made no sense. Given the book's modern English, the author's claim of having traveled back in time, and the description of the astrolabe as a broken time machine, João decided he would have to take a closer look at it. But just then he had an idea. *This place is big enough for all of us to spend a month or so collaborating on our project, a project that just might involve a specially modified spherical astrolabe!*

CHAPTER THREE

THE INTERVIEW

PROGRAM HOST: "Good morning to all you fabulous listeners of Hawaii's oldest student-run public radio station, KTUH Mānoa, the station that loves you! I'm your host, Mojdeh Molavi. I'm a grad student in the Middle East Studies Department. Today we have a special treat for you. With me in the studio (a very nice seminar room, I might add) are Professor Aisha Hidayat, chair of the Indonesian Studies Department, and six newly retired faculty members; in fact, they all retired this year. Professor Hidayat will be interviewing them after I briefly introduce them. I promise that you'll be blown away when you hear about the amazing project they're about to embark on! Here they are:

"Professor Sandra Bevilacqua taught in the UH Political Science department. Professor Abbas Amir taught in our Anthropology department. Professors Yuen Ho Wan, Horacio Fuente and Makelle Ringhiera were members of the History department faculty. And Professor João da Gama had a joint appointment to the History and Geography departments.

"Now I'll turn it over to Professor Hidayat."

Aisha Hidayat: "Thank you Ms. Molavi. I know this will be a particularly interesting program for you because your PhD dissertation will deal with the same regions and historical periods as our guests.

"I have known them all professionally for many of the 30 years they've been on the faculty. Some of the disciplines they've taught and researched at the University included the histories of Africa, the Middle East, and China. They're fluent in Arabic. I find it fascinating that the common denominator, so to speak, in their professional studies is the city of Mogadishu. So, without further ado let's start with the gentleman who has brought all of you together, Professor da Gama. Professor, why don't you tell us what brought you all together."

João da Gama: "Thank you, Professor. My colleagues and I have worked closely with one another at various times during our 30 years here at the University. What we're involved in now is an in-depth, multifaceted study of 15th century Mogadishu, Somalia. Mogadishu was then, and still is, the capital of Somalia, which occupies the so-called Horn of Africa, north of East Africa. And when I say `multifaceted,' I mean `in person' as well. During our project, we'll be traveling to that war-torn city. I'll tell you about my part in the project after you hear from my colleagues."

Aisha Hidayat: "I'm quite sure we'd all like to hear more about that trip in a few moments, to tell us about your particular part in this project. But first I'd like to introduce my other guests. Professor Sandra Bevilacqua is a world-renown expert on the 15th century, in particular relations between Mogadishu and Persia. She also has written about the warfare in the Mediterranean between the Ottoman empire and the Italian States. She was born in Italy and graduated with honors from the University of Milan. She earned a PhD from UCLA and joined the UH Political Science Department 30 years ago in 1989. She recently published an article on the political structure of Mogadishu's government in the early 1500's.

"Professor Abbas Amir's specialty is the history of Arab-Somali relations in the Horn. He grew up in San Francisco's Arab community and graduated from San Francisco State. After graduation he took two `gap' years off from school so he could travel throughout the Middle East. Then he went to grad school in Egypt and earned an MA from the American University of Cairo. Next came a PhD from UC Berkeley. He taught in the UH Anthropology Department for 30 years. He has written extensively on the cultures of the Horn of Africa in the late 1400's.

"Professor Yuen Ho Wan was born in Hong Kong. His family emigrated to California when he was 10. He graduated with a double major in History and Chinese languages from UCLA. He received a PhD from Stanford, specializing in the China-Africa relationship over the centuries, especially the 15th and16th centuries. Professor Yuen also joined the History Department 30 years ago. His doctoral dissertation was on the legendary fleet of "Treasure Ships" commanded by the Chinese maritime admiral Zheng He, who made seven voyages throughout the Indian Ocean. Professor Yuen has published several articles on the Treasure Ships' visit to Mogadishu in the 15th century.

"Professor Horacio Fuente began his studies at the University of Porto, Portugal, when he was 16; probably a record for the youngest freshman there. He broke another record when he earned a PhD at the University of Hawaii when he was 24. His dissertation dealt with Arab and Portuguese relations with East Africa in the 15th and 16th centuries. He published extensively on that subject throughout his career. While still a grad student working on his PhD dissertation, he joined the History Department first as a lecturer 30 years ago when he was 22. He was appointed assistant professor two years later when he completed the PhD, and associate professor two years after that. His post-retirement plans include completing a study of the growth of Islam in Mogadishu in the late 1400's, as well as a study of Somali-Abyssinia-Portuguese relations during that period and beyond. He is working with Professor Makelle Ringhiera on that.

"Professor Makelle Ringhiera was born in Harar, Ethiopia. He did his undergrad work at Berkeley and his PhD at NYU. He joined the History Department 30 years ago. He has researched and written extensively on relations between Somalia, Ethiopia and Eritrea, especially in the 1600's. He is a renowned scholar in Arabic, Somaliña, Amharic and Tigriña. He is working on a history of the northern Somali port city of Zeila and is collaborating with Professor Fuente on Somali-Abyssinia-Portuguese relations at that time.

"Professor João da Gama earned his BA and MA degrees at the University of Washington and his PhD at the American University of Cairo. During his 30 years at UH he had a dual appointment in History and Geography. He had published extensively on Portugal's 15th and 16th century explorations of Africa. His current research is a study of maritime navigational systems, in particular the different types of astrolabes such as the spherical astrolabe.

"So, let's start with Professor Bevilacqua. Professor, can you give us a brief introduction to the city of Mogadishu and what you plan to write about?"

Sandra Bevilacqua: "Certainly. Listeners might be surprised to hear that Somalia wasn't always the fragmented, violent failed state that it is now, with Mogadishu ground zero of much of the fighting between clans and the Somali government, such as it is. In the 15th century the city had a stable government ruled by a Sultan. Somalia had trading relations with other African communities as well as India, Arabia, Persia and even China. Since my particular specialization was and is Persia, it was natural that my contribution to this group's project would be Persia's relations with the Horn of Africa."

Aisha Hidayat: "Professor, you said China had relations with Somalia back in the day. Perhaps I should ask Professor Yuen Ho Wan to enlighten us on those relations. I know that you, Professor Yuen, have written extensively on the voyages of the Chinese 'Treasure Ships' of the 15th century. I am a bit of an amateur historian on them, ever since I learned that one or more of those voyages visited Sumatra, where I was born."

Yuen Ho Wan: "Yes, the phenomenon of the Treasure Ships has fascinated me ever since my undergrad days. It's one of the subjects I wrote extensively about during my career. Zheng He was a Chinese Muslim eunuch working for the Ming dynasty Emperor Yongle. In 1405 Admiral Zheng He launched the first of seven voyages west from China across the Indian Ocean. Over the next 30 years, in command of the world's largest fleet, he explored Southeast Asia, India, the Persian Gulf and the east coast of Africa. Many of the vessels, built at the shipyards of Nanjing, were equipped with such innovations as watertight compartments in multiple hulls, sternpost rudders, magnetic compasses and paper charts and maps. The ships were packed with fresh water and food supplies. There were also Chinese luxury goods intended to woo foreign rulers into displaying their appreciation of the Ming dynasty's obvious wealth and power by sending back to China some of their own riches in tribute. Chinese historical documents show that the fleet was estimated to have between 20,000 and 32,000 expedition members, including diplomats, medical officers, astrologers and military personnel."

Aisha Hidayat: "And what in particular will you be focusing on in your collaboration with your colleagues here?"

Yuen Ho Wan: "My research will be an in-depth continuation of my long-term study of the Treasure Ships. Historians have suggested that the Admiral's fervent desire was to round the southern tip of Africa, explore the west coast of Africa and go further west. But to do that, he knew he would need much more sophisticated navigational tools. So, I'll be examining the historical record to determine just how far the Admiral got in his quest. I'll be getting some input from Professor da Gama on the type of navigational tools Zheng He had access to."

Aisha Hidayat: "Before we ask Professor da Gama to enlighten us about his research into the spherical astrolabe, let's hear what Professor Abbas Amir is up to these days."

Abbas Amir: "Thank you, Dr. Hidayat. My contribution to our group's project will be an in-depth study of the many cultures in and around Mogadishu in the 15th century. Because of the city's strategic trading location on the Indian Ocean, just below where the Red Sea comes out near Djibouti, there were many cultures represented in Mogadishu. There were Somalis, of course, but also Arabs, Indians, Persians and other East Africans. I hope to provide some more detail as to that cultural mix. I will be collaborating with Professors Fuente and Ringhiera."

Aisha Hidayat: "Thank you, Dr. Amir. Professor Fuente, why don't you provide the listeners with the scope of your plans for this investigation into 15th century Mogadishu."

Horacio Fuente: "Well, as Professor Amir mentioned, I'll be working closely with him and Professor Ringhiera on the many cultures present in the region at that time. My particular hope is to shed more light on the full extent of the Portuguese presence in Somalia in the 15th century. The historical record is replete with documentation on the Somali-Abyssinian war of the 16th century, a war in which the Portuguese participated on the side of the Abyssinians. But less documentation exists as to the full extent of Portugal's presence in the region. Professor Ringhiera is an expert on Abyssinia and, in addition to his ongoing research into the history of the Somali port of Zeila, his expertise in the various languages of the region will enable us to hopefully provide a more complete portrait of the Horn of Africa."

Aisha Hidayat: "Thank you, Professor Fuente. Let's hear from Professor Ringhiera now."

Makelle Ringhiera: "Well, as my friend and colleague has just mentioned, he and I and Dr. Amir will be expanding the understanding of the cultural diversity of the Horn. My additional contribution will be to examine the Abyssinia-Portugal relationship in the 15th century. As perhaps you and your listeners know, the Abyssinians at that time tolerated the Portuguese for a while. In fact, they relied on Portuguese help in repelling the invasion of the Somali warlord Ahmad Grañ in the 16th century. But after that, the

Portuguese were essentially 'shown the door' because of their persistent attempts to convert the population to Catholicism."

Aisha Hidayat: "That's interesting. I understand Grañ came very close to overrunning the Abyssinian highlands. I'm sure we all wonder what would have happened in the Horn had Grañ been successful, or if the Abyssinian emperor had allowed the Portuguese to remain.

"Well, let's return to Professor da Gama and learn a bit more about this fascinating group effort you all have planned."

João da Gama: "Thanks, again, Dr. Hidayat. As you mentioned, my particular academic interest in geography included an inquiry into the impact the marine navigational instrument known as the spherical astrolabe had on world exploration and commerce. Certainly, the device was a relatively new phenomenon in the 15th century, largely introduced by the Portuguese explorers of the Indian Ocean all the way to China. One of those remarkable devices almost literally fell into my lap a few months ago. Not only that, but apparently accompanying the device were several documents dating back several hundred years, most importantly a book written in the 15th century in Mogadishu.

"Our group will be using the documents and the astrolabe to supplement our historical inquiries into the Horn of Africa and the city of Mogadishu in particular.

"To do that, of course, we've decided to work together on this project and our own individual projects. About nine months ago, I had the opportunity to buy, renovate and staff a one-hundred-year-old, 16-bedroom mansion on the island of Molokai. It's a beauty, I have to say, with more than enough bedrooms and living rooms for our whole group as we work as a group and individually."

Aisha Hidayat: "Can you tell us more about the book and documents? That is so amazing that you should find them in an old mansion. Were they written in Arabic or Somaliña? And how did they come to land in Hawaii, all the way from Mogadishu?"

João da Gama: "Well, because these things just came into my hands so recently, I want my colleagues to have a good look at them first. More information on their contents will be forthcoming as our research progresses."

Aisha Hidayat: "I understand, even though I, and I'm sure our listeners, are eager to hear more about your discovery.

Before we let you go, a listener has emailed a question: `Since you all retired at the same time, how did that impact the academic programs you worked in?'"

João da Gama: "Well, in our careers, each of us of course taught and wrote about a number of different academic topics. Early on, as our research brought us closer together on the subject of the Horn of Africa in the 15th century, we naturally began collaborating. Our respective departments supported our collaboration, and have been very diligent in hiring new faculty who would carry this research forward."

Aisha Hidayat: "Thank you so much for enlightening us on the history of this most important area of history. I hope we can have you back on this program in the future. Good luck in your research and writing!"

As the group left the KTUH studios Makelle said, "I can't wait to see the 500-year-old book! Not to mention the accompanying ancient documents."

Sandra said, "I second that. When you talked us into moving into your mansion and collaborating on an historical project, you didn't say anything about finding the astrolabe, book and docs."

"You'll just have to wait. It'll be an incredible experience, I guarantee it." When they got to their cars, João added, "So, it's goodbye for now; see you in a month, or sooner if you can get away!"

CHAPTER FOUR

SHOW TIME

For the next several weeks João was busy putting the final touches on the upcoming arrival of his guests. He spent a lot of time working with the kitchen, housekeeping and janitorial staffs on their duties. A month ago, he had hired another cook, two servers, half a dozen housekeeping staff, a bookkeeper and half a dozen janitorial staff. He realized that he was trying to keep as busy as possible, so he wouldn't have time to be depressed over the death of his wife a year ago.

He couldn't help but compare himself to the lord of Downton Abbey, even though it was a completely new experience for the retired professor. Not only had he spent most of his adult life teaching college students and doing research, he had never had the kind of responsibilities he was carrying out now. Nor had he ever had the resources to buy this abandoned 19th century mansion on Molokai, not to mention the resources to renovate it and hire cooks, servers, housekeeping staff and janitorial staff. His wife's life insurance payout provided for everything and more.

Not only was João working overtime with the staff and the remaining tasks related to getting the mansion ready, he was very nervous about how to present his discovery of the spherical astrolabe and ancient documents to his colleagues. *At least I gave them a heads up during the radio interview. But still, they are about to have their minds blown!*

Over the past year, he had been lucky in his research into the history of astrolabes, especially the spherical astrolabe. By keeping a close eye on current notices of museum downsizings and estate sales, he was able to purchase half a dozen of the type of spherical astrolabe he had found in his attic. Now he had plans for those machines given what the book said. He was looking forward to sharing what he was sure would be an amazing experience for everyone.

João didn't have to wait the full month for his colleagues to join him on Molokai. Makelle Ringhiera was leading the caravan of his friends' cars driving slowly and carefully along the gravel road through the center of the island on the southern coast. It was midmorning when they passed by the main town of Kaunakakai and arrived at João's mansion.

João was standing on the large front porch as his friends parked, got out of their cars and stood staring at the mansion. João laughed and yelled out, "I'm thinking of naming it `Starlight'; what do you think?"

"Why Starlight; does the roof leak that badly?" Yuen asked.

By then the group had reached the front porch. João chuckled and said, "Come on in and get comfortable. Then I'll fill you in on the name."

Although it was a sunny February morning in the low 70's, the huge, high-ceilinged parlor was still chilly and a little damp. João had built a fire in the main fireplace but that didn't completely dispel the chill. "You can drop your bags on that side table there. Then have a seat; I'll give you a tour of the place in a minute."

João walked over to a large, gorgeous steamer trunk and opened the lid. He lifted out a smaller wooden/brass chest and a leather briefcase. To João's guests, both items looked to be antiques. He brought the chest and briefcase to the coffee table in the center of the room.

"You all may recall me telling you about the six attics in this place.

I finally got a look into each of them and cleaned them out. Mostly they were empty, except in one there were boxes of books and this trunk. I have to say I was never more surprised than by what I found inside it."

Makelle walked over to the trunk and was examining it closely. "How in hell did you manage to wrestle this out of an attic, for God's sake?"

"I had help, of course. I had my gardeners rig up a rope basket and lower it to the master bedroom. They then brought it downstairs."

Abbas said, "That chest and briefcase look downright ancient. What do you estimate their age to be?"

"Actually, they're not really ancient-ancient; just 50 or 60 years old. They didn't belong to the elderly gentleman who sold me the mansion. He had said somewhat apologetically that he didn't have the time or energy to completely empty the house. I'm pretty sure these items had been in the attic before even he bought the house. I don't think he knew who put them in the attic and when."

Sandra said, "I'm dying to see what's inside them."

"Well, I'd like to give you a tour of the rooms first, then we'll have lunch cooked by my wonderful cooks. THEN we'll have a look at the amazing things inside the chest and briefcase. First, let's walk upstairs to the third floor. I'm sure we could use the exercise, and I don't think we should all try to squeeze into the ancient elevator."

On the third floor were the master bedroom and bathroom, eight smaller bedrooms, a reading room, two bathrooms and the antique and very unreliable-looking elevator. The second floor consisted of two dormitory-style staff bedrooms and bathrooms, four wardrobe closets and two closets full of brooms and cleaning supplies. The ground floor contained the parlor, the dining room, two sitting rooms—one facing the front of the mansion and one facing the back—, a sun room on the side, a library and kitchen. An auxiliary kitchen was in the basement, along with a dining room for the staff.

Adjacent to the staff dining room was a closed doorway. In his tour of the mansion, João didn't open that door. He wasn't quite ready to show them see his huge science lab—reagents, jars of miscellaneous powders, a jar labeled "gold wire," a jar labeled "platinum wire," a jar of semiprecious gemstones with holes drilled through them, coils of solder, butane torches, soldering irons, jeweler's drills, and assorted other tools. But the main things he wanted to avoid showing them just yet were the spherical astrolabes.

Once João had led the group back into the parlor he said, "Well, do you like my mansion? Later you can decide which bedrooms you want. They all look out onto the grounds and all have heating grates over the ducts leading from the furnace in the basement."

Abbas asked, "Before we do that, are you going to tell us the order of business to get us started on our collaborations?"

"Patience. Let's have lunch first. I want you to be well fed and a little drowsy when it's showtime."

"Drowsy? Why drowsy?" Sandra chuckled.

"Maybe I don't want you to be too argumentative. Just passive and accepting of my presentation."

Yuen raised his eyebrows and said, "Are you expecting arguments?"

João and the others laughed. Just then one of the cooks came out of the kitchen and announced lunch.

CHAPTER FIVE

THE "STARLIGHT COMMUNE" IS BORN

Lunch was a lively affair. The group of University of Hawaii faculty friends were eager to get going on their various research projects and the overall collaboration they would be undertaking in this intensive study of the Horn of Africa and Mogadishu in particular. As they walked around the parlor admiring the carpets, the walnut paneling, the genuine gaslight chandeliers, and the paintings of exotic Middle Eastern scenes by Jean-Leon Gerome. One painting by Stefano Bonsignori of the Horn of Africa was something no one was familiar with. Makelle stood in front of it and asked, "Who is Stefano Bonsignori and when did he paint this?"

João said, "He did lots of paintings of the Middle East and Europe in the 16th century. He was a fairly obscure priest or monk at the Vatican. He passed away in 1589."

João didn't seem to be in any rush to get down to business. "First, before we get started, why don't you all go upstairs to the third floor and put your stuff in the bedroom of your choice. No fighting! Then come back down and let's have our meeting."

Once they were back downstairs and seated comfortably, João opened the briefcase, removed two items and set them on the table. The first was a packet of papers. The second was the strange-looking book bound in black leather with two words embossed on the cover, one on top of the other. They were in two languages everyone in the room was familiar with. Pointing to the word "ግራኝ" on top, João said, "This is the word `Grañ' written in Amharic. The word 'عراني' below it is Arabic, and also means `Grañ.' Anyone want to venture a guess as to what that word means?"

Makelle raised his hand. "It means `left-handed' and refers to the Somali warrior Ahmad Grañ of the 16th century, the man who almost conquered Abyssinia. He fought with a sword in his left hand."

Sandra said, "Why would a leather-bound book have the word `Grañ' embossed on the cover?"

The question stumped everyone.

João sat back down. Turning to Horacio he grinned and said, "The cover's reference to Grañ is particularly puzzling since the book was handwritten in the middle of the 15th century by a Mogadishu resident named Horacio Fuente."

Horacio smiled and looked around at the group, "I bet you all never knew about my famous ancestor." Turning back to João he said, "He must have been a Portuguese would-be colonist or missionary who had been kicked out of Abyssinia."

João continued, "Who knows? The author doesn't say anything about Abyssinia."

In the meantime, Yuen, who had been leafing through the packet of papers, said, "Some of these papers are written in Chinese. Where did these things come from?"

João said, "I found the papers with the book in the briefcase. Some are in Chinese, some in Somaliña. The papers written in Somaliña, which I can read, appear to be some sort of journal written by a Harari nobleman in the 16th century."

After a few seconds, Sandra said, "Back to the cover of the book. Why `left-handed' if the author doesn't talk about Ahmad Grañ?"

"The author says nothing about the cover. I've examined the cover pretty closely, and I suspect it was pasted onto the original cover later. Nor does the author say anything about Ahmad Grañ. But that's understandable since the book was written before Grañ came on the scene in Somalia."

Sandra continued, "Have you read the book?"

"Yes, I have. Several times. It's part autobiography, part instruction manual. But as you can imagine, it's very fragile. I'll say more about it in a second. For now, I want to show you what's in the wood-and-brass chest." He walked to the chest, opened it and removed an object wrapped in what looked like a Kilim rug. He walked back to the coffee table and set the object down.

All eyes were on the Kilim as João carefully unwrapped it. A spherical astrolabe mounted on a small pedestal sat on the table. To most people it would be a very strange object. But this was something almost everyone in the group had seen before, or at least had seen pictures. João said, "Anyone want to tell us what this is?"

Abbas said, "It's an unusual-looking spherical astrolabe. It looks remarkably well preserved. The ones I've seen in museums and private collections all showed signs of wear and even damage. I can't imagine why the astrolabe was inside the trunk along with the book and journals."

"At first I couldn't either. When I found the trunk in the attic it seemed to be full of books. It wasn't until I had it brought downstairs that I was able to empty it out. The smaller chest with the astrolabe, book and journals was underneath the books."

Everyone came closer and walked around the table. Sandra said, "So, did the book explain why the briefcase containing the book and papers were in the trunk with the astrolabe?"

João said, "No, the book described the spherical astrolabe in some detail, but said nothing about the papers. The papers written in Somaliña don't say anything about the astrolabe. Maybe the Chinese papers can tell us who the author was and why they were in the trunk with the astrolabe. But I haven't read them because I don't read Chinese. Yuen, now that you've taken a look at the papers, does the author says anything about the astrolabe? Maybe it didn't belong to the author."

After a few minutes Yuen said, "Apparently the author was a lifelong Chinese diplomat. These papers are his memoir. Mostly he was talking about his many postings—Harar, Mogadishu, Djibouti, Cairo, Milan, Portugal, Hawaii."

João said, "The real estate agent told me the man who sold me this mansion was a descendant of a diplomat who had traveled all over the world. Maybe these things belonged to the diplomat. Strange that the seller would leave these things in the trunk. Maybe he didn't know the trunk was in the attic. If he knew about it, maybe he thought the trunk was just full of books and never bothered to empty it. Maybe the astrolabe belonged to the diplomat as well. What does his memoir say about the book and astrolabe?"

"The author of the Chinese memoir doesn't say anything about the book except that he took it with him everywhere for good luck. But he said he bought the astrolabe in Oporto, Portugal from a maritime museum that was selling off its collection of nautical navigation instruments."

Once again, João looked surprised. "That's consistent with what the book says about the astrolabe. I was saving the best part for last, so get comfortable. I'm going to read you a short excerpt from the book. Here's what the author says about the astrolabe:

"*The strangest thing about having found myself in Mogadishu was that it seemed to be a different Mogadishu than the one described in history books. Be that as it may, soon I no longer wanted to return to my former time. This Mogadishu is now my home. My beautiful astrolabe, had I not fallen and broken something inside it, might have made another journey to another time, but I will not go with it. My daughter Alessandra will send it off to whatever destiny awaits it. I was fortunate that Alessandra could ensure a pre-ordained future for my spherical astrolabe. When I told her what my history books had said about the date the fleet of Vasco da Gama would anchor offshore Mogadishu, we formulated a plan where she would hire a fishing boat to take her there and present the astrolabe to the Captain. I will remain here, rooted in the past, living in a wonderful city, married to a wonderful woman and father of a wonderful daughter.'"*

Silence. And more silence. Just when Horacio was about to speak, a cook came into the room and said afternoon tea would be served in the sun room.

Once again, the friends found themselves sitting around a table. Only this time there was no laughter, no lighthearted chatter. Finally, Horacio spoke. "What did the author mean by `make another journey to another time" and `rooted in the past'? Or `pre-ordained future?' It sounds like he's describing time travel."

João smiled and said, "That's exactly what he meant. The answers to those questions are in the spherical astrolabe itself. I'll fill you in when we're finished with our tea."

When the group returned to the parlor and had taken seats on the comfy couches, João said, "Before I continue, let me make a suggestion. Since we're going to be living and working here for some time, allow me to propose a name for our group. Humor me. How about we call ourselves the `Starlight Commune'?"

Sandra said, "Why Starlight?"

Makelle said, "And why Commune?"

"The spherical astrolabe was once the marine navigation device that revolutionized global exploration. It used the stars and planets so much more effectively than the older astrolabes. According to the book, this machine here was modified to use the planets and stars themselves to travel through time. If we learn how this particular astrolabe was modified, how to use it as intended, and modify five more like it, we will truly have become a commune traveling under the power of the heavenly bodies. I know you want to hear more so let me tell you more about this device and take a closer look at how it works."

CHAPTER SIX

THE SPHERICAL ASTROLABE

João picked up the astrolabe and said, "Follow me." He walked to the stairway and walked down to the basement with the rest of the group following. João opened the door to his lab. Before motioning for the group to follow him inside he said "This is my workshop. I'll explain what we're going to have to do to our astrolabes."

Abbas said, "You said our astrolabes. Are you assuming we're going to find more?"

João said, "I've spared you the trouble. Look." He motioned the group into the lab and pointed to the long table in the middle of the lab. Six astrolabes identical to João's were arranged around the table, and in front of each was a tall laboratory chair. "I got lucky and found six astrolabes in museum sales in Los Angeles and San Diego. That's right. Using Google, you can find anything and have it shipped via air freight anywhere in a matter of days." João set his own astrolabe down on the workbench.

The five other charter members of João's just-created "Starlight Commune" immediately started moving around the table and examining the machines. After a few minutes Yuen turned to João and said, "Okay, let's get on with the demonstration. What will you do with the astrolabes, and why?"

João smiled. "We're going to follow the directions in Horacio's book and turn these astrolabes into time machines. This one I have is already a time machine, but I won't be traveling anywhere with it. The book is very clear that when a group of time travelers activate their machines together, they must remain together or else none of the machines will work. The book explains that when they are energized together, they must remain together. Since the astrolabe I found in the attic had apparently been part of another group, it will probably no longer function. For now, I'll just use my machine to illustrate the instructions in the book. Maybe we'll visit Mogadishu! We all would just love to get to know 15th century Mogadishu up close and personal. Of course, nothing may happen at all and I'll have egg on my face! We'll see."

Crickets. João's laugh broke the silence. "I was expecting scoffing and scowling, but not stunned silence!"

Sandra said, "You know, João, you're saying this book is talking about building a time machine. If this Horacio guy traveled back in time, who built the time machine he used? Where is it now? Is that it on your workbench? All this sounds like science fiction."

"First answer—yes, the book is talking about a time machine. Second answer—the book doesn't say who built Horacio's machine. Third answer—Horacio's machine is probably this spherical astrolabe right here, because it has been modified according to the instructions in Horacio's book. It even had a broken silver wire inside this globe that's suspended in the middle, just as the author described. I opened the globe up using the tools here in this lab, and I could see that the modifications followed the book's instructions to the letter. I soldered the broken wire, something the author said he wasn't able to do in the 15th century. What he might have done if he hadn't broken his astrolabe is impossible to say. The book is silent as to whether he traveled alone or with a group."

Abbas said, "Let's back up for a second. This Horacio guy, does his book say where he came from?"

"No, nothing. The book is all about his life in Mogadishu, how happy he is, what a great place it is, how he loves his wife and daughter. It's almost as if he wanted to leave his present life in the past. Or his past life in the future."

Sandra said, "Wait a minute. How could anyone, especially someone who is apparently a Westerner, love Mogadishu? The place is a hell hole, everybody knows that."

João said, "Well, that's how it is now. Who knows what it was like in the 15th century? The only contemporary accounts of Mogadishu in the 14th and 15th centuries were written by Arab travelers who didn't say much other than the city was prosperous. No description of the people except to say they were `nomadic in character.' Think of how great it would be if we could come back with enough material to write books, many books!"

Horacio said, "You know, João, I don't think any of us, except apparently you, believes time travel is possible. You say the book describes the astrolabe as a time machine." Smiling and looking around at his companions, he sighed and continued after a long pause, "Well, what the hell, what's the worst that could happen? Let's see what these babies can do!"

"I intend to do exactly that." Without saying anything more, João picked up a long, slender forceps-like tool. He carefully inserted it between two of the flat silver bands that formed an orbit around the insides of his astrolabe. Then he grasped the top of a hinged, orange-size golden globe that was sitting on, and soldered to, a `hammock' of silver wires attached at both ends to the bands. A single silver wire appeared to pass through a hole drilled in one side of the bottom half of the globe and out through another hole drilled in the other side. Squeezing the forceps, João opened the top of the globe. There was a bed of thin wires resting on the bottom of the globe. "The book says those thin wires are made of platinum."

The single silver wire that passed through the globe had been threaded through a small gemstone inside the globe. The gemstone was suspended by the wire above the bed of platinum wires. That silver wire then passed through the hole drilled in the opposite side of the globe. The wire was soldered on both ends to one of the flat silver bands that orbited the inside of the astrolabe.

Withdrawing the forceps, João set them down on the workbench and looked at the others. Pointing at the little globe, he said, "The network of wires, my friends, was constructed according to the instructions in Horacio's book. He doesn't say where the instructions came from. The book says the globe was originally hollow, like the globes inside these other astrolabes. It describes in detail how these four silver wires must be soldered to the bottom of the globe and then soldered on both ends to the flat silver bands that encircle the globe. The directions explain that those four silver wires hold the globe suspended in the center of the astrolabe.

"The book also explains how this single silver wire here must pass through one of those holes in the bottom of the globe, then be threaded through the gemstone, suspending it above the bed of platinum wires. Then it exits the globe. Each end of the silver wire must be soldered to this flat silver band orbiting the astrolabe.

"To create that configuration in these other astrolabes, we would have to first lay out a bed of platinum wires on the bottom of the globe. Then we would use the tiny jeweler's drill to make a hole through each side of the globe. Next, we solder the silver wire to this silver band on one side of the astrolabe. Then, after carefully threading the wire through the first hole, we thread the gemstone onto the wire. The instructions say you have to make sure the silver wire holds the gemstone suspended above the bed of platinum wires.

"The silver wire exits the globe on the opposite side through the hole you drilled there. Then you solder the wire to the flat silver band on the other side of the astrolabe. The fact that solder is used shows me the modifications were not made in the 15th century, because solder hadn't been invented yet.

"Once you've completed that very complex operation, you're done. I have to tell you, I'm damned if I know how anyone could have come up with this idea. But apparently the idea worked. This gentleman says he traveled back in time to Mogadishu courtesy of the spherical astrolabe."

Sandra frowned. "He says he ended up there, courtesy of this gadget. But there's no proof."

João said, "Well, he also describes how to activate the thing."

"And how does one activate it?" Sandra scoffed.

"I was just going to get to that. Not activate it, of course, but tell you what the book says to do. We're not going to try it until all of us are ready for our maiden voyage."

"Wait, wait," Makelle said. "You're assuming we're going to convert them according to the instructions in the book. Have I got that about right?"

"You've got that exactly right. Come on, where's your sense of adventure? Aren't we all getting a little bored now that we're retired? Aren't we all itching to do something exciting, like visit Mogadishu in the 15th century? Think about the numerous books and journal articles you'll write describing Mogadishu!"

Makelle laughed, "Look, I grew up in the Horn of Africa, Harar to be precise, and I would imagine Mogadishu would be several orders of magnitude scarier than Harar. Maybe in the 15th century it might be paradise, but I doubt it."

João smiled and said, "Let's go back to the parlor where we can discuss this in comfort."

CHAPTER SEVEN

CURIOSITY WINS THE DAY

Sandra's skepticism notwithstanding, she apparently was becoming more enthusiastic about the project, "Well, let's get this show on the road! What's the worst that could happen? We'll end up sitting around with expensive toys sitting on our laps." The others chuckled and nodded.

When everyone was seated in the parlor João asked, "You all came here expecting to spend a month or two researching and writing about the Horn of Africa. Are you all okay with spending part of your time here playing scientist?"

Sandra said, "Well, Mr. Impresario, maybe you've forgotten something. What about the components that go inside the gold globe?"

João said, "I have all that stuff already—silver wires, platinum wires, gemstones, gold and silver solders."

Horacio said, "What kind of gemstones, and how will the silver wire pass through them?"

"Maybe you noticed the small jar of gemstones in my lab. They're emerald-green chrome tourmalines. Although they're rare, and therefore expensive, I found a jeweler in Kuanakakai who sold me six 7-millimeter stones for $100 apiece. He drilled each of them for another $10 apiece. So, a total of $110 apiece."

Yuen asked, "Why this particular gemstone?"

"It has magnetic properties, and is also thought by many indigenous Hawaiians to remove energy blockage, similar to how yoga and tai chi facilitate energy flow in the body."

This seemed to induce a period of silence. Makelle said, "So, why don't you tell us what we'll be doing with these machines? And then what comes next?"

João said, "Here's the plan. Tomorrow morning bright and early, we take our seats around the work table. I'll pass out a tray of components and a pair of forceps to each of you. Then I'll demonstrate the process. But for now, I think we need to pause and spend the evening talking about some ideas I want to run by you."

The "Communards" didn't go right in to dinner. There was a lot to think about. Makelle suggested they take a walk around the grounds and have a late dinner afterwards. Nobody disagreed. João suggested they walk to the top of the rise behind the mansion; he wanted to show them something. It was not a particularly strenuous climb, and when they got there, they were rewarded by a by a dark blue sky gradually filling up with stars. Sandra said, "I love the starlight. You never see a clear night sky full of stars in the city."

Makelle pointed out what appeared to be very ancient moss-covered stones set in a semicircle around the top. João nodded and said, "I suggest we take a seat on these stones and admire the starry sky. These stones have a certain, what shall I say, attraction, especially in starlight. But more on the subject after dinner."

When they walked back to the mansion, they proceeded directly to the dining room. They took seats around the table and chatted before the first course came out. Once dinner was underway, João said, "You know, I wasn't joking when I suggested we ought to consider taking a trip back to 15th century Mogadishu. I know each of us has studied and written about the Horn and the Swahili Coast. But we've also run up against a wall when it comes to really getting to know the region. And it's not just a problem of language because most of us read Arabic, one of us also reads Ethiopian and Somali languages, several read Portuguese and one of us reads several Chinese languages. The problem is probably that there weren't very many chroniclers around then. What I propose is we get `up close and personal' and write about it."

João held his breath as he waited for a reaction.

Abbas said, "Aren't you jumping the gun here? You have yet to demonstrate how to activate these astrolabes, let alone 'program' them, so to speak, to deliver us to a particular time and place."

"You're right. After we make some progress modifying them, I'll explain how Mr. Fuente of Mogadishu fame says to activate them."

"And what about the return trip, so to speak?"

"Fuente explains how to do that as well. Patience, my friend."

CHAPTER EIGHT

AT THE WORKBENCH

After breakfast the next morning, João led them downstairs to the workshop. The first thing João did was point out that he had already had each gold globe cut and hinged. Then he demonstrated how to open the hinged globes with the forceps. It took the Communards several tries before they could perform this seemingly simple act on their own astrolabes. João smiled finally and said, "Congratulations! Now that you're reasonably skilled at manipulating the forceps, you're ready for the next step, the nest of platinum wires!"

Once everyone began, João walked down the bench and observed the friends as they laid the bed of nine platinum wires on the bottom of their globe. That was a meticulous, time-consuming process. Then he supervised them as they began drilling a tiny hole in each side of the globe with their jeweler's drills. João cautioned them to "go slow; you want to get the hole in exactly the right place on each side of the globe so that when you thread the silver wire through the holes, the wire will follow a straight path between the silver bands on either side of the globe."

By then they were exhausted from the intense focus of attention to detail. João supervised each of them, one at a time, to make sure they drilled the holes correctly. It was almost noon when they finished that task, and appetites began making themselves known.

After a leisurely lunch, João suggested they take a dip in the two spring-fed hot tubs he had installed behind the mansion. "You'll need to relax a bit, especially your hands. The next task requires a certain amount of dexterity."

There was no argument except for Sandra, who said, "I'm sorry, but I didn't bring a bathing suit. You didn't say anything about a hot tub."

"Don't worry. I keep a supply of bathing suits for my guests. Actually, you all are my first guests."

By 3 o'clock, the group had enough of hot water and were ready to get started on the next phase. Once they had showered and changed, they proceeded to the laboratory. João said, "For this task you'll use the little soldering iron to attach the silver wire to one of the silver bands that circle over and under the globe on the inside of the astrolabe. You'll then carefully insert the wire through the hole you drilled on one side of the globe. You'll lay the wire temporarily on the bed of platinum wires to get it in position for threading it through the gemstone. After you've threaded it through the gemstone, you thread it through the hole on the other side of the globe and lay the wire down temporarily as you get ready for the next task. It's important that we do this step very carefully.

"Whoever thought up these modifications was careful to explain that what he or she had done was `program' the modifications so they would `point' to the chosen geographic and temporal destination. In the case of this particular astrolabe that I found in the attic, the geographic destination was programmed for Mogadishu and the temporal destination the year 1430.

"Here's how the programming was done. You'll notice two long silver arrows extending across the inside of the astrolabe from one side to the other. One arrow passes a few inches above the golden globe and the other passes a few inches below. A broad, doublewide silver band forms an orbit just inside the top and bottom bands of the astrolabe. According to the book, that band is actually two independently movable bands. Each can be rotated so that the arrows point to a specific geographic destination. But the owner of this machine modified it so that each band could be rotated so that one arrow points to a geographic location and the other arrow points to a location in time. If you look closely, you'll see pairs of numbers etched on one band along its entire length. Those are geographic coordinates that mariners used to orient themselves as they sailed the oceans. But the gold-soldered numbers you see on the other band were added later. Those are dates. When you line up a date with a location, you have your time-travel destination. So, what we're going to do with these `virgin' astrolabes on the bench is make the modifications that will energize them."

Sandra, ever the skeptic, said, "When you say energize, what do you mean?"

"I mean the modifications we'll make to the inside of the golden globe will, according to the book, `energize' the configuration so that it can be activated to transport the user to the selected place and date."

Yuen said, "Maybe now is the time for you to explain exactly how we'll activate this thing."

"Very simple, really. You place one hand on the bottom of the astrolabe where the crossed arrows begin their journey to the other side, and the other hand on top of the astrolabe where the arrows end. Then you say a prayer, and get ready for an `A Ticket ride' to the past."

As instructed, the group soldered the silver wire to the silver band on one side of the astrolabe. João guided them as they ran the wire through the first hole, threaded it through the gemstone, and passed the wire out the other side of the globe. By then they had to take a short break to give their hands a rest. When they were ready, João guided them as they gently pulled the silver wire taut in order to lift the gem off the bed of platinum wires. They then soldered the silver wire to the flat silver band on the other side of the astrolabe.

"It's almost dinner time. You've all done an amazing job! Let's take a dinner break and then we'll talk some more about what we'll do once we've arrived in Mogadishu. Tomorrow morning we'll talk about preparations for the trip."

CHAPTER NINE

GETTING READY

The Communards sat around the dinner table discussing the astrolabes with a certain amount of trepidation. Horacio said, "I'm not sure what exactly we're going to do in Mogadishu in 1430, assuming these machines actually work. For one thing, Mogadishu was, according to the Arab travelers who visited the city in the 15th century, a large city on the coast of Somalia. What if these machines transport us off shore, into the water? Or into the no-man's-land outside the city?"

"That won't happen, according to the book. This spherical astrolabe that the author used transported him to an alley on the edge of the large open-air market, the '*Suq*,' as they're called all over the Middle East. I assume our machines would do the same. And to return we would regroup at that alley and hold the astrolabes the same way we did when we started."

João could see that the friends were warming to the idea.

Makelle said, "What about money? They didn't use paper money. I presume we'll have to mint our own coins. But the coins that have survived from that era are too worn and damaged to give us a clear idea of what the coins looked like or what denominations existed. And clothes—we'll obviously need to be dressed like the locals." The others nodded in agreement.

João smiled and said, "We're gonna go shopping tomorrow in Lahaina, Maui. It's an hour and half by ferry each way. Even if you've never loved shopping before, you're gonna love this trip! First, we'll go to the jeweler I found in Old Town who'll sell us small pieces of gold, silver and copper, which he already will have pounded into one-gram size coins. I figure we each should bring half a dozen gold coins, a dozen silver coins, and two dozen copper coins in case we find stuff to buy. I hope you remembered to bring some cash; this gentleman doesn't take cards or checks. The price he quoted for each of us is $260 for the coins. And then we'll hit the flea market on the outskirts to look for Middle Eastern or African garb—robes, headgear, and such."

Yuen said, "And we'll obviously have to buy something to carry the machines in; backpacks, carpet bags, something."

João said, "Yes, we'll look for leather or canvas satchels that we can sling over our shoulder; those were common in the 15th century. Girdle purses to carry personal effects were also common."

The six of them climbed into João's SUV and he headed for the ferry terminal. Once in Lahaina, they wasted no time and headed directly for João's jeweler. The gentleman, a middle-aged native Hawaiian, was ready with the coins. "Might I ask why you're buying coins like these?"

João said, "We're academics headed for Africa. We'll be trekking around in some pretty remote places, places where the people don't use the national currency. Barter, amber, gold, silver, copper are the customary forms of buying and selling."

The jeweler seemed surprised, but nodded his head. "It must be a pretty remote region. Still, I've heard of such places. My nephew was in the Peace Corps in southwest Ethiopia where the people hardly ever used paper currency. Well, good luck on your trip."

The gentleman started to put the coins in a bag, but Sandra said, "I think we should buy six of those small leather pouches you have in the display case and carry the coins in them." The jeweler took out six pouches and laid them on the counter. The group divided up the coins into the pouches, paid for their purchases and left the shop.

As the group strolled through the festive town, Yuen said, "There's an older district not far from here where there are several second-hand shops. Some Chinese, Indian and Arab people on Maui still wear traditional garb. We'll probably find what we need in those shops. Maybe we'll find some kind of satchel to put our astrolabes in."

After three hours combing through the merchandise at the second-hand shops, everyone had purchased robes, sandals and keffiyehs; everyone except Sandra. She was adamant that she would not wear a veil, or traditional Muslim women's clothes. She found a calf-length tunic and bought two. "I don't have to pretend to be an Arab or even a Muslim. I've read about Somalia in those days, and it wasn't as homogenous as it is now. Besides, with my dark hair and olive complexion, I could pass as Indian."

As they passed what looked like a traditional dry goods store on the outskirts of Lahaina they decided to go inside and look for something resembling a satchel. They were lucky. Hanging on hooks in between shelves in the back of the store they found many canvas bags meant to be carried over the shoulder. They were big enough to accommodate an astrolabe. They also bought small leather pouches for their personal effects.

They were finally ready to return to Molokai. João said, "The last ferry back leaves in an hour and a half. Let's stop and have a cup of tea before we get on board. The tea on the ferry is awful."

CHAPTER TEN

DEPARTURE

The companions spent the evening discussing what they thought they would need for the excursion. Horacio said, "Do we know what we should be looking for? Of course, we should try to talk to people but I would imagine our accents and manner of speaking will make people nervous or mystified."

Makelle said, "I think what we'll be looking for are things like the types of buildings, streets, shops, merchandise. Document all of it. And of course, make note of the diversity of the people themselves. I'd imagine we'll see Arabs, Indians, Africans, Persians, just about every ethnic group. Even Chinese. Now that I recall, Admiral Zheng He's fleet visited Mogadishu for the last time in 1430."

Abbas said, "What a great opportunity! I would love to see the fleet. Maybe one of the smaller vessels will be docked so we can get a good look. I doubt his 'treasure ship' could dock anywhere near the shore. Probably be a mile out with one or two smaller craft docked and taking on supplies. It's interesting, though, that the spherical astrolabe in João's attic was programed for the exact year of Zheng He's last visit to Mogadishu."

Yuen frowned and said, "We aren't going anywhere near the ships. Nor should we approach any Chinese sailors we might see. Maybe some of you weren't aware of Zheng He's history of abducting people to work on his ships. He was always looking for such folks as translators.

"As for what to bring, we should bring notebooks, sketchpads and such. Remember, folks—we're not going on vacation. This will be a working trip. If these astrolabes actually work, we'll be face to face with enough historical material to write any number of groundbreaking articles and books."

João made sure everyone was up at the crack of dawn. "I hope everyone's packed and ready. We're going on a short hike back up to where we went before, our `embarkation point' so to speak."

Sandra said, "Why there? Why not set up the astrolabes on the grounds here?"

João paused before answering. "I don't have a scientific reason, just a superstitious attraction to those ancient stones up there. Humor me. So, let's get our stuff ready and get going."

It didn't take long for everyone to do one last check and assemble on the porch. As they began walking up that little hill their feeling of anticipation grew. Finally, they reached the semicircle of ancient stones that directed their gaze out across the Pacific and beyond.

"Here's what I propose. Each of us will stand in front of a stone so that we're all looking out across the Pacific toward Japan. Then we'll activate our astrolabes simultaneously. And say a prayer."

Everyone stood in front of a stone holding their astrolabes in front of them. When they were all facing Japan, João said, "Okay. Everybody ready? Put one hand under your astrolabe so that the bottom end of the arrow rests on your palm. Hover your other hand just above the tip of the arrow, but don't touch it. On the count of three, lower that hand and touch the tip of the arrow. Either the astrolabes will send us back in time, or we'll be standing here looking foolish. And remember—remember!—we have to stay together and return together. These machines will probably no longer function if they are ever separated by time!"

Three seconds later the group did as João instructed. Immediately the view across the brilliant blue Pacific turned two-dimensional and gray. The view undulated, and it seemed as if they were looking through wavy glass in an antique window. Then the view dissolved and reconstituted itself as a tunnel or alley, dark on one end and bright on the other. They were no longer standing in front of ancient stones on Molokai looking out across the Pacific. They were standing in an alley with buildings on either side of them. The buildings appeared to be two stories high. At the back of the alley, they could see empty crates and broken carts. In front of them was a crowded street or walkway. They could hear a cacophony of sounds— shouting, laughing, music, braying of donkeys. They were halfway down the alley from the entrance.

Sandra said, "I'm gonna go out on a limb here and hazard a guess—we're in the Mogadishu public market. I hear Arabic and Somaliña. But hold on—I think I hear Portuguese! That can't be right."

Horacio said, "I hear it also, which is very strange. I didn't think Portuguese had arrived in East Africa by 1430; unless this isn't really 1430. Well, let's not just hang out in this alley. Let's mingle and find out where and when we are!"

CHAPTER ELEVEN

GOING SHOPPING

Everyone put their astrolabe in their shoulder bag. With Horacio leading the way, the group walked out of the alley. They were standing at an intersection of two streets of highly compacted dirt. The streets looked like they had recently been sprinkled with water to keep the dust down. It looked and felt to be about noon, and the heat and humidity were uncomfortable. People and carts were moving in all directions all around them.

"These damn flies!" João pointed to several meat stalls. "There's the culprit. Let's move away from here and look for an area that sells dry goods, pottery, pots and pans, that sort of thing."

They walked slowly through the market. Suddenly João held up his arm and said, "Stop. I can't believe what's up ahead on the right. Could that be a church?"

Abbas said, "That's certainly a church, not a mosque, as you would expect in Mogadishu."

Yuen said, "I suppose it's possible there's a community of Christians here, perhaps from missionary efforts. But, as Horacio and Sandra observed, nothing in the history books mentions churches in Mogadishu."

Sandra said, "Well, let's move on. I feel like trying out my bargaining skills, not to mention my Arabic." She stopped at a stall that sold leather goods—belts and sandals, primarily, but also bags and pouches. She picked up a beautiful lambskin drawstring pouch embroidered in silver and gold thread. She tried out her Arabic. "This is very nice. How much?"

The merchant was a young woman who looked to be Somali, judging by her height and coffee-colored complexion. She seemed to be surprised by what Sandra asked. Sandra switched to Somaliña. "I said this pouch is very nice. How much is it?"

The woman smiled. "I think I understood you at first, although your Arabic is the very formal type that I'm not very good at. I am Somali, born here. This purse my uncle made himself. He told me not to accept less than 5 silver taler."

The others in the group watched the transaction from a few meters away. Sandra said, "I'm sorry but I've only recently arrived here and I'm not sure of the currency. I only have coins from my country." She reached into her purse and took out a silver coin. "Is this about 5 silver taler?"

The young woman took the coin and examined it. "I'm afraid I've never seen a coin like this. Let me weigh it. I'm pretty sure it doesn't weigh enough." She turned and brought a scale to the counter. She placed the coin on one side of the scale and a local silver 5-taler coin on the other. "Put another of your coins on the scale and let's see if it weighs the same." After doing so, it appeared two of Sandra's coins were sufficient and the sale was complete.

The group continued their stroll through the market. By then it was early afternoon and they were hungry. "Let's look for a food stall," Abbas said. They stopped in front an open-air cafe or bar.

João said, "Okay, it's my turn to try out my Arabic. The man behind the counter doesn't look Somali; he looks like an Arab." The group entered the cafe and João asked the proprietor if he spoke Arabic. The man registered surprised but answered, "I haven't heard formal Arabic very often. Most people speak the colloquial version. But you look Portuguese. I'm Portuguese also, from Oporto." Smiling, he switched to Portuguese. "What can I get for you and your friends?"

João was stunned. "Yes, I'm Portuguese. But I didn't know there were any Portuguese in Mogadishu."

"Yes, we have a growing community. That's our church just up the street. So, what would you like?"

They ordered broiled lamb on rice. The clerk was surprised by their coins, but the sale was soon consummated. They sat around a table in the shade and tried to decide what to do next. Horacio said, "I don't know about you, but I'm gonna buy a beer if possible."

Sandra said, "Get a pitcher and mugs. We're all thirsty and this spicy lamb is only gonna make us thirstier."

Horacio brought back the beer and mugs, poured out beers for everyone, and got down to the business at hand—eating and drinking.

In between bites, João said, "Anyone want to explain how it is that this clerk is Portuguese? And his church while you're at it? We all know, or at least we thought we knew from our studies of history, that the Portuguese didn't arrive in East Africa until many years from now." No one had an answer.

Makelle looked up after a few minutes. He looked around and said, "Do the rest of you smell the salt air? I'd bet we're near the port."

Yuen frowned and sighed. "Let me repeat—we should steer clear of the port; the Admiral's ships might be docked and we'd be in danger should any of his sailors spot us."

João said, "But why would they necessarily take an interest in us? Don't we look like everyone else?"

Yuen said, "No, we don't. You and Horacio look Portuguese, and as Horacio and Sandra said earlier, there shouldn't be any Portuguese here. Sandra looks Persian. Makelle has the classic looks of an Ethiopian. Abbas is the only Arab among us. And if a Chinese sailor spotted me, a Chinese man, he might just come over to check us out."

The group finished their meal and resumed their stroll through the market.

Horacio motioned for them to stop. "Look at that shop—looks like it sells manuscripts and maps." He was intrigued; he'd been hoping to find medieval maps and even a manuscript or two. He went inside while the others waited outside.

As he was browsing, he heard Abbas yell, "Horacio, get the hell out; we've been spotted. Run, back to the alley!"

He dropped what he'd been examining and stepped out of the shop. He looked to his right and saw his companions running down the street with two Chinese sailors in fast pursuit. Horacio ran after them but wasn't sure how close he should follow. A few seconds later, he saw his companions enter the alley where they had arrived. "Oh shit! I hope they manage to make it back home." Horacio ducked behind an unattended coach and hid, keeping an eye on the alley. After a minute or two he saw the two sailors come back out of the alley scratching their heads. They walked away and turned onto a side street.

Horacio muttered, "Now's my chance, maybe my only chance." He took off running toward the entrance to the alley, all the while keeping his eye on the side street where the sailors had gone. As he ran, he looked from side to side to make sure he wasn't spotted. Just before he got to the entrance to the alley his friends had turned into, he stumbled and fell. His satchel and astrolabe broke his fall. He jumped up again and entered the alley. He quickly pulled out his astrolabe and put his hands on it to activate it.

Nothing! Again, he tried it. Nothing. Crouching down behind an empty crate so as not to be seen, he carefully examined the astrolabe. He didn't see anything that appeared to be broken, but when he shook it, he heard a rattle coming from inside the gold globe. He tried once more to activate the astrolabe but nothing happened.

"Shit! Goddamn it! Now what?"

CHAPTER TWELVE

TRAPPED!

Realizing he could not remain in the alley for much longer, he cautiously walked out into the street, keeping an eye out for any sign of danger, such as the Chinese sailors from the treasure ship. He walked briskly in a direction he hoped would lead him away from the center of the market and toward an area where he might find some kind of lodging. As he walked past the Catholic church they had passed before, he tried to remember whether the accounts written by the two 15th-century Arab travelers had said anything about churches. He was pretty sure they hadn't; the city was uniformly described as a city of many mosques and a few small Hindu temples, but no churches. He muttered, "How could those visitors have overlooked this?"

He walked for almost an hour before he saw what he hoped was an inn. He wasn't sure, though, because the building didn't look like the traditional type of inn consisting of a tavern on the ground floor and rooms in the floor above. This building was much larger and in the shape of a huge horseshoe. The bottom of the horseshoe was directly in front of him and faced the street. There was an open door in the center.

He entered and was shocked at the size and opulence of the room, which was apparently the lobby. On the right was the entrance to what looked like a dining room. To the left was a bar or tavern.

There were a few men sitting at tables in the tavern. Directly in front of him, in the middle of the lobby, was what he hoped was the registration desk. Horacio decided to see if he could get a room.

He was surprised to hear the desk clerk speaking Portuguese to someone, apparently a guest. Feeling relieved, he spoke Portuguese to the clerk and asked about a room. "I wasn't sure this was an inn until I heard you speaking to that guest. Is there a room available?"

"Yes, we have several on the second floor on my right. One room looks out onto the street and the other has a view of our garden."

"I've never seen an inn in the shape of a horseshoe. And I didn't expect to see a Mogadishu inn as large as this, or one with a tavern inside."

The clerk smiled and said, "Yes, it is pretty unusual. Years ago, it housed the government of the Sultan. But when the Sultan moved his offices to a new building at the Port, this building lay vacant for a year or two. The father of the present owner bought it and converted it to an inn. By the way, my name is Manolo. I'll be glad to show you around the inn."

Manolo asked his assistant to watch the desk and said, "Let me show you the rooms I mentioned." Horacio followed Manolo up the stairs. When they entered the hall, Manolo said, "Each arm of the horseshoe has a hallway 40 feet long and 10 feet wide. Each of the arms has three guest rooms on the first and second floors. Let me show you a very nice room available at the end of this hall. It's away from the noise of the tavern below and has a view of the huge garden in between the arms of the horseshoe."

Horacio was shocked when Manolo told him how little the room rented for. The room rented for a pittance. Horacio realized that with the gold, silver and copper coins in his pouch, he would be able to stay there for many months or more. *I can't let that happen. I have to get the astrolabe fixed!*

Horacio said he would take the room, went inside, set his bag down and stood at the window looking down at the garden. Turning away from the window he tried to collect his thoughts so he could prioritize his tasks over what he hoped would be only a few days.

He knew he should put the astrolabe in a secure hiding place, but for now he placed it under the bed. Then he realized he would need to buy clothes and an extra pair of shoes. He was wearing his only shoes, and they were sandals. Before he made the trip back in time with the others, he wore clothes that he hoped would make him appear to be an Arab. His outer garment was a light cotton *jalabiya* commonly worn by Arab men. Under that he wore loose-fitting sweatpants and a plain white tee shirt. He would also need to buy writing materials, and hopefully some sort of tools with which he might be able to reattach the silver wire inside the gold ball in the astrolabe.

But before he set out, he sat down on the small bed and surveyed his new home. The mattress looked and felt like it might be stuffed with straw. He hoped it was bug-free straw. On the bed there was a thin, threadbare blanket; he hoped there was a sheet underneath. Next to the bed there was a desk and chair. Opposite the bed there was a basin mounted on the wall with a pan and jug of water on the floor. What looked and smelled like a chamber pot was under the bed. On the wall above the desk was the window looking out onto the garden. *Well, I could be worse off, I suppose.* With that optimistic thought, Horacio lay down on the bed and fell asleep even though it was barely getting dark. It was the first day in his new home.

Horacio awoke a few hours later to the sound of exotic music from the tavern below. It sounded like a blend of Middle Eastern and African. He thought he could hear some kind of stringed instrument, as well as a flute or other wind instrument, a bit of percussion, and someone singing; a man's voice lamenting the state of the world, or maybe a longing for a lover. He decided to venture downstairs and grab a bite and something to drink. And listen to the music. The room was not crowded at all, probably because of the late hour; he thought it might be midnight.

A few minutes after he sat down at a table, the waitress approached and asked if he would like to order a beer. He had assumed he would have to settle for tea or fruit juice. He was surprised to hear the waitress speak to him in a form of Arabic he could barely understand. Trying out his somewhat formal classical Arabic, he ordered a beer and a dish of fish and rice.

"Well, well, I see you are a very educated man. I can barely understand your Arabic. We mostly speak a more colloquial form in Mogadishu." She sounded like she had a Portuguese accent. Horacio had thought that the only Portuguese in East Africa arrived in the 16th century far away in Abyssinia and they were Jesuits. She looked like she could be in her mid-fifties. She was beautiful.

Horacio said, "I can barely understand colloquial Arabic. By any chance do you speak Portuguese?"

Her smile widened and she said, "Yes, as a matter of fact I do. I was born in Oporto, and came here with my father, who was one of the first Portuguese traders to arrive. How do you know Portuguese?"

Setting aside his astonishment that a Portuguese person, a woman no less, was working in a tavern that served an alcoholic beverage in a Muslim city, Horacio found himself making up a fairly interesting life story. "Iwas born in Sagres and lived there until my mother died when I was 10. My father took me with him to the Maghreb, in Northwest Africa. He was a shopkeeper, and I was his assistant. Most of the people there were the Berbers. Even though Arabic was not spoken much around the proud Berber people, my father insisted I learn formal Arabic and put me into the local madrassa. As it turned out, I was very fortunate that he did that, because I learned my letters and mathematics. Since we were Portuguese and not Arabs, my father's business was moderately successful. When my father died, I sold his shop, travelled east and eventually made my way here. I just arrived this morning."

"Oh, it sounds like we have something in common. My father also insisted I go to school and learn mathematics and to read. I learned Arabic when we came to Mogadishu, but the colloquial version." Sitting down at the other side of the little table, she smiled and said, "My name is Mariana. And I assume you are Christian."

"Yes, I am Christian. Mariana is a nice name. My name is Horacio. Pleased to meet you."

The beer was strong and dark, but with a completely unknown taste. The fish-and-rice dish was fresh and spicy. When Mariana returned at his signal for another beer, he asked, "I am looking for clothes and shoes. Can you recommend a nearby shop?"

She smiled. "Yes, I can recommend a very good shop that sells all manner of men's clothing."

"Thank you. That would be very helpful. By the way, you said you came here with your father. Is he the owner of this wonderful inn?"

Mariana sighed and said, "No, he isn't any longer. He owned it for over 10 years and trained me as his business partner."

"I don't mean to be nosy, but I hope your father is still with us."

"I hope and pray he's still alive. He said he was going to make a trading journey down to Mombasa. But it's been almost 3 years since he left, and he was already almost 70. Before he left, we transferred ownership of the inn over to me. Even though I miss my father terribly, I am enjoying being an owner of a prosperous inn."

Horacio hated to end this most pleasant conversation, but he was going to be busy soon. "Well, I also hope he's still with us. And I hope he will return soon a very wealthy man. Now about those directions—Oh, in addition to clothes, I wonder if you can tell me where there might be a nearby shop that sells paper, writing materials, that sort of thing."

"Are you a writer or a scribe? I can help you find clients."

"That would be wonderful. In fact, that's exactly what I would like. But I would have to write in Portuguese or formal Arabic rather than colloquial Arabic. I don't imagine there are many Portuguese in Mogadishu."

Mariana looked surprised. "Oh, but there are. I 'm sure I can find clients for you. Now let me get some paper and a pen." Mariana walked back into a room behind the bar and returned with two quill pens and half a dozen sheets of paper.

Horacio picked up a quill pen, examined it closely and then picked up a sheet of the paper. "This is a very fine quill. And the paper is smooth and absorbent. Where can I buy these things?"

Mariana smiled and said, "I must close the bar soon. When I do, I can show you the street of bookshops and such things. Also, the street where you can purchase clothing and shoes."

"Oh, that would be wonderful. You have been most kind."

By the time Horacio finished his second beer and another plate of fish and rice, the last patron had left the inn. He stood and walked to the bar. When Mariana came out of the back room, he said to her, "I have one other favor to ask of you. I have a nautical instrument that I need to have repaired. I wonder if you can keep it safely in your office while I search for someone who can repair it."

Mariana smiled and said, "Yes, certainly. I have a strong box in the closet at the back of the office. There is room in there. But I 'm afraid I cannot help you find such a repair shop. Perhaps tomorrow on your quest for shoes, clothes and writing materials, you will come across such a shop." She smiled and proceeded to clean and straighten the tables. Horacio helped her, much to her surprise.

Finally, she closed up and the two of them walked a short distance to a street that appeared to have nothing but clothing shops. "Tomorrow, after you look on this street for your clothing needs, just go a little farther in that direction, turn left, and you will be on a street where you can purchase paper, pens, books and everything else. If you get lost, just ask for the *'sharie aleulama'*. I am very happy you are staying at my inn, Horacio, and I look forward to helping you."

The next morning dawned bright and warm. He brought his astrolabe downstairs and Mariana stowed it in her strongbox. Then she served Horacio a delicious hunk of fresh bread, a generous slice of soft cheese and a small glass of tea. When he had finished eating, she walked with him to the front of the inn and reminded him of where to go for his shopping needs. "Oh, I remembered just now where you might be able to find someone to repair your instrument. After you are finished with your purchases, just go another few hundred yards past the street of books and such, turn left, and I think you might see such a shop there. At least, that's what I seem to recall."

Horacio enjoyed his walk to the clothing shops, where he had no trouble purchasing what he needed. He enjoyed actually using the Arabic he had learned during his years of academic study. Many of the shopkeepers were familiar with formal Arabic. He bought two pair of short linen breeches, a belt, a doublet, and a pair of woolen hose to cover his legs. The hose had leather soles and he could wear them without shoes or boots. He bought another pair of hose without the leather soles, a pair of fine riding boots and three pairs of woolen socks.

He also found a shop where he bought paper, ink and quill pens. He even noticed a bookbindery and made a mental note in case he wanted to gather his notes into a book. But just thinking such thoughts depressed and frightened him. *I must not let myself think I will never find a way back home!*

He was becoming very comfortable in his new, hopefully temporary, home in Mariana's inn. He was aware that he projected the image of a middle-class academic of some sort. That was fine with him. Mariana soon found him clients who needed documents prepared, and he began tutoring local children in Portuguese grammar and composition.

But the difficulty he was having in finding someone who could repair his astrolabe was more and more troubling. Horacio assumed that, because of the booming mercantile economy in Mogadishu, most artisans discovered they could live more comfortably as merchants buying and selling than working as artisans. At first, he thought it would be extremely difficult to perform soldering on something in such a confined space. But after he purchased several books on metal work in general, he remembered that in the 15th century soldering hadn't been invented yet. In one book he read that "the pieces to be joined are joined by introducing a copper salt in and around the joint and heating in an open fire till the work 'flashes' meaning when the copper salt is reduced to copper by the fire and locally drops the melting point of the surface." That hardly sounded like an operation that could be carried out in the tight confines of an astrolabe. And, frankly, Horacio worried about his astrolabe being damaged or stolen should he leave it with an artisan to be repaired.

In the meantime, Horacio spent his time tutoring, preparing documents, and writing in his journal. He gave up studying different ways to reattach the broken wire in his astrolabe. After a few attempts at locating a bookbindery, he found a shop that could bind as many as 70 or 80 pages of paper into a book with leather covers. He began writing a journal and found that he was beginning to feel more and more like Mogadishu was his home.

CHAPTER THIRTEEN

A NEW LIFE

As the weeks turned to months, and then to years, Horacio continued to work as a tutor and as a scribe for merchants needing letters, wills, and other documents beyond their abilities. His friendship with Mariana blossomed into love, and they married in the year 1434. Despite their ages—67 for Horacio and 54 for Mariana—they had a daughter, Alessandra, born in 1435.

Horacio soon confessed that he had been a time traveler. At first Mariana didn't t know what to believe about time travel. She had never heard of it. But when Horacio told her about his group of academic friends in a place called "Hawaii" in the distant future, something in the way he described his past life convinced her he was telling the truth. She wasn't hurt that Horacio had deceived her; she trusted him and was fascinated by his stories.

CHAPTER FOURTEEN

DECISION TIME

And they were gone… from Mogadishu… to the hill top on Molokai.

"Where the hell is Horacio?," Sandra said, looking around. "Could he still be in Mogadishu?" They were all a little shaky and disoriented. "I don't know what happened. Everything seemed to work out fine. Except this. Horacio was right behind us, running from the Chinese sailors. He wasn't with us when we reached the embarkation point, but I had hoped he would catch up. Oh, God. I hope he wasn't taken prisoner."

João said, "Let's go back inside and think about this." They walked slowly back down the hill to the house.

After everyone had taken seats in the parlor, João walked to the table, picked up the book, and returned to the circle. "I'm guessing now that the Horacio who wrote this book was our own Horacio Fuente. Certainly, the prefatory note in front suggests that. He came to terms with the reality that he would never return to his home. But the 70 pages in this opus attest to the happiness he enjoyed throughout the remainder of his life."

Sandra said, "Well, despite our extremely brief time in 15th century Mogadishu, we learned something new. We now have confirmation of what Horacio said in his book: The Mogadishu we visited was not the same Mogadishu we studied in history. We saw

Portuguese people. All the historical documents I've come across state that the Portuguese didn't arrive in East Africa until the 16th century, and they were in Abyssinia, not Somalia. We saw churches. No mention of churches in Mogadishu. We saw the ready availability of alcohol in what our history books said was a Muslim city."

João said, "I suspect that even if we could return to Mogadishu, it would be yet another Mogadishu than the one we visited just now. That's even if our astrolabes could make another trip to the past, which, with the loss of our colleague, would not be possible, according to the book."

Makelle asked, "What's our next step? Our plan?"

Yuen asked, "More specifically, what do we do with our astrolabes?"

Abbas said, "Don't forget the book. What about the book?"

Sandra said, "Here's my suggestion. We remove the section of the book with the directions for converting the astrolabes into time machines. And then we restore the astrolabes to the way they were before we changed them."

There was a period of silence before João said, "Well, allow me to be a devil's advocate here. Let's suppose we do what Sandra suggests, change the book and restore the astrolabes. But that won't change the fact that Horacio, our Horacio back in the 15th century, wrote his book chock full of instructions for making a time machine. And not only that, he couldn't do anything to fix his astrolabe, so he arranged for his daughter to give it to Vasco da Gama. Who knows what the Great Navigator did with it."

Makelle laughed. "You're a pretty good devil's advocate, my friend. Allow me to add something. Suppose someone will find Horacio's book. Maybe Ahmad Grañ, in one of his military campaigns in Somalia, will find it and put his moniker on it, so to speak! And maybe someone will find da Gama's spherical astrolabe in some museum. Maybe that someone will build a mansion on Molokai."

There was laughter, but the laughter died quickly.

CHAPTER FIFTEEN

A VOYAGE FOREORDAINED

A Phenomenon in Padua, 1455-1460

Mariana Mendes and her husband Horacio Fuente turned away from the dock where the caravel Kamaluddin was anchored and began walking back into town. It was an early morning in July, and the day promised to be a hot one in Mogadishu. Despite their ages—Horacio was 87 and Mariana was 75—they were in fairly good health. Neither was overweight. They got plenty of exercise and worked 12-hour days in a busy inn in the busy Hamar Weyne district of Mogadishu.

Mariana had the copper complexion of a Portuguese woman who had spent almost her whole life in the harsh light of Somalia. She had brilliant green eyes and curly dark brown hair that refused to turn gray. She was so tall that her clients and acquaintances liked to accuse her of being Somali. When she got pregnant at age 54, she had to create the myth that the women in her family all conceived in their 50's.

Horacio was 67 when Mariana became pregnant. He was not surprised that he wasn't sterile. He had maintained a healthy vegetarian and seafood diet. He spent part of each day walking to the small office he maintained near the Port. He kept to a daily exercise regimen. As a result, he was slim and energetic. Like Mariana, he was tall with curly, dark brown hair and copper-colored skin.

Just now they had delivered their 20-year-old daughter Alessandra to the ship that would take her on the first stage in a lengthy trip that would eventually take her to Italy. The first stage would be sailing northeast along the Somali coast. The caravel would then make a sharp left turn and enter the Gulf of Aden. Soon the ship would pass through the narrow Bab-el-Mandeb strait. From there the ship would sail north and slightly west up to the top of the Red Sea. The caravel could go no further at that point and would dock at the Port of Suez. Alessandra would take a coach overland to Alexandria, Egypt. Then she would book passage on a caravel to cross the Mediterranean and travel up the Adriatic Sea to Venice. After a short coach ride, she would arrive at the University of Padua. As far as her parents knew, she would be the first female student at the University.

Mariana had owned and operated the prosperous Funduq Mendes inn for 25 years. She grew up in Mogadishu from the age of five. Before that she, her parents and aunt and uncle had lived in Oporto, Portugal. Mariana's parents and aunt and uncle had jointly owned a successful export-import business there. But Mariana's parents decided to leave Oporto when it became too congested. They immigrated to Mogadishu and opened up a new export-import business. Their business flourished in that beautiful, multicultural city. Merchant ships arrived almost weekly from all over the Indian Ocean, as far as China to the east and as far as Mombasa to the south. There was caravan traffic all over the Horn of Africa as far west as the Abyssinian highlands.

When Mariana's mother died, her father sold his business and bought the former official office building of the Sultan's government after the Sultan moved his government to new offices at the Port. Mariana and her father converted the building to an inn and named it Funduq Mendes. Mariana became the sole owner after her father failed to return from a business trip to Mombasa. Three years later, she met Horacio. They married in 1434 and Alessandra was born a year later.

Having a newborn baby and trying to run a popular and busy inn in a large city proved to be very difficult for Mariana and Horacio. When Alessandra was two years old, Mariana decided to ask her sister and brother-in-law, Catarina and Gonçalo Lopes, and their two-year-old daughter Beatriz, to come and live with them. The Lopes family arrived six months later in early 1437. In exchange for their generous agreement to pull up stakes in Oporto and move to Mogadishu, Mariana made them full partners with her and Horacio.

When Alessandra and Beatriz were little girls they thrived in their "jobs" as the inn's official goodwill ambassadors. The girls looked so much alike that the guests and townspeople at first thought they were sisters. They were tall and had a tanned olive complexion typical of both Portuguese and Somalis. They were fluent in Arabic and Somaliña. Their green eyes and straight light brown hair, however, definitely set them apart from Somalis.

As they grew older their responsibilities in the inn grew proportionally. They learned many of the tasks of inn employees— waiting tables, cooking, cleaning guest rooms, and eventually some bookkeeping. But the majority of their time was spent in school. Between the ages of six and 15, they attended the local Catholic school. They studied mathematics, science (chemistry and physics), Portuguese, and religion. From among the electives, Beatriz studied formal bookkeeping. Alessandra studied astronomy. After graduation, their parents enrolled them in the local private school that Horacio had set up catering to the local foreign community. Its curriculum included instruction in Italian and English.

When the girls graduated from that private school four years later, Beatriz decided to pursue a career in management at the Funduq. Alessandra decided to apply to the University of Padua in the Venetian Republic. She had strong interests in Astronomy and Languages. She and Beatriz understood that they would someday inherit the inn upon the deaths of their parents and become partners.

Horacio had begun his second career working as a notary, scribe, translator and teacher by the time Alessandra was born. He was quite successful and gained a reputation throughout the city as an honest and talented professional. He did that for the next 20 years, retiring when he was 86, a year before Alessandra's departure for Padua. During his career in Mogadishu, he wrote a book full of stories of the city and region.

The part of the book he was most proud of, however, was the way he came to Mogadishu from 500 years in the future. He titled the book:

From the Future to the Past
by Dr. Horacio Fuente,
Professor of Near East History (ret.),
University of Hawaii.

Horacio entrusted Alessandra with his book to keep it safe and deposit it in an archive somewhere after her graduation from the University. He hoped Alessandra might someday have a family and would retrieve the book and keep it as a family history.

He also entrusted Alessandra with the device that had brought him back in time from the 21st century, a modified—but now broken—spherical astrolabe. Her instructions were to attempt to offer the astrolabe to the Portuguese explorer, Vasco da Gama. Horacio knew from his studies of history that da Gama would anchor off Mogadishu in the evening of January 2, 1499, and depart the next morning without entering the city. Should Alessandra succeed in giving the astrolabe to da Gama, Horacio hoped he would use it for many years before donating it to a Catholic monastery in Portugal. He would be unaware of the modification to the astrolabe.

As they walked, Mariana looked around at her city with pride and love. Then she brought her mind back to their daughter. "We can't do any more than what we've done already. The rest is up to her. I hope you're right that she will lead a… what did you call it, a 'charmed life'?"

"Yes, charmed in the sense that she has a destiny, a key part to play in seeing that my spherical astrolabe ends up in a place where it will become a quaint conversation piece."

Mariana said, "I feel bad that we've kept the truth from her before now. I mean the real truth, the truth of what happened when you travelled back in time to this version of the past. I do hope you make sure she learns the whole truth when she returns from the University."

"Of course. I'll explain it all to her when it's time to do so."

"You say she'll learn the real story when she returns from the University. But after you tell her the real story, won't you tell her she'll have to modify the book where it talks about the astrolabe?"

Horacio said, "Definitely." He paused and looked around at his beautiful adopted city. "Why don't we walk back to the house? I feel like walking, not looking for a carriage. We can talk about how I think the astrolabe and book will make their way back to the future."

The two of them continued on toward the Hamar Weyne district of Mogadishu where they and Alessandra had lived since her birth in 1435. Mariana said, "I still worry that this thing that brought you here, the spherical astrolabe, will be lost or stolen. There are bound to be many stages in its long journey back to the future, each more perilous than the earlier stages."

Horacio still didn't answer. Mariana understood the history of his device. She knew that it had been transformed from a sophisticated mariner's tool for navigating the oceans, to a sophisticated tool for traveling through what Horacio called "the interstices of time." That tool had brought her husband to her.

She also knew, despite her husband's suggestions to the contrary, that on some deeper level he still missed his prior life. He occasionally sobbed at night. Maybe she wanted to hear him repeat his story so she could experience his love for her all over again.

Horacio pointed to a small grassy area next to the city's main mosque. "Let's sit down in the shade. This heat and humidity are harder on me than they used to be." They found a shady spot under a tree. Horacio, sitting cross-legged like a Sufi master, said, "Here's my short version of the paradox, a fortuitous paradox for me, you and Alessandra." Horacio took a breath and delivered the story he had told Mariana, Alessandra and the Lopes family many times. "My colleague at the University of Hawaii in 2018, João da Gama, found a trunk in the attic of a dilapidated mansion he bought on the island of Molokai. Inside the trunk was a 500-year-old book written in 20th-century English. The book was written longhand by a man who gave his name as Horacio Fuente, which amused João because that was the name of one of his colleagues.

"The largest item in the trunk was an ancient mariner's tool, a spherical astrolabe. It had several silver bands and wires crossing from one edge of the astrolabe to the other. One of the wires appeared to pass through a small golden globe in the very center of the astrolabe. But according to Fuente's book, the wire had become broken inside the globe. The book provided instructions on how to repair the astrolabe and restore it as a time machine. But that was impossible with 15th-century tools and knowledge.

"João and some colleagues searched for other astrolabes in the hope of converting them to time machines. In the 21st century spherical astrolabes had long since been replaced by modern nautical navigation instruments, and could only be found in museums or private collections. Eventually, João's group was successful in acquiring several.

"Following the instructions in the book, they converted them to time machines and travelled back in time to Mogadishu in the early 15th century, their academic specialization. But the powerful Chinese Admiral Zheng He had his fleet of 'treasure ships' in port. Horacio's group had studied the history of Zheng He's numerous voyages from China to ports in India and Africa. They knew that Zheng He was notorious for kidnaping people with skills that might benefit his ships. The group decided to return to the 21st century to avoid capture. As they were running back to their `navigation point,' Horacio fell. His fall broke a wire inside the astrolabe. It could not be repaired by then-current technology. He was stranded in the past, married a wonderful woman named Mariana, and they had a wonderful daughter named Alessandra.

"Horacio very quickly learned that this Mogadishu he was stranded in wasn't the historical Mogadishu he had studied extensively in his academic career. It was what he called a `parallel' Mogadishu. That meant that he, the parallel Horacio Fuente so to speak, must make sure that his spherical astrolabe would remain nonfunctional."

Horacio stopped to catch his breath.

Mariana said, "I think this is tiring you out. Let's get up and continue to our home."

The Imam's Introduction

Mariana and Horacio stood and brushed themselves off. A young imam had just come out of the mosque and started walking along the path in their direction. As he came up, he smiled and greeted them. "Salam alaikum."

Mariana responded in Arabic, "Wa alaikum Salam. Are you one of the imams at the mosque?"

"Yes, although a very junior one. My name is Abdullah Assad."

"Pleased to meet you. My name is Mariana Mendes and this is my husband, Horacio Fuente. You must be very pleased to have a position at such an important mosque as this. I wish you good fortune in your career."

"Thank you, but I won't be here for long; I'm due to be transferred soon."

Horacio said, "Oh, I'm sorry to hear that. I hope you'll be transferred to a prosperous mosque in a quiet town somewhere. Don't you find life here in Mogadishu a bit hectic and busy?"

"That's true, but on the other hand it's a very interesting city. Such diversity of people—Arabs, Indians, Africans, Persians, even Europeans! The city I'm being transferred to is quite far north, near Djibouti."

Mariana asked, "Are you talking about Zeila?"

"Yes! That's right. Do you know anything about it?"

"Only that it's a charming small city on the coast. I visited it once with my parents. What's the mosque like in Zeila? Small? Large?"

"I'm told it's the main mosque in the city; a large one. With a large, well-maintained library and archive. In fact, my duties will include taking over and reorganizing the archive."

Horacio put his right hand on his chest and addressed the imam in his somewhat academic Arabic, "That's wonderful! I'm sure you'll enjoy your new post. Muslim history in East Africa is very rich. You will find your position to be a very important one. I'm certain God will smile on you and grant you many successes in your career."

The young imam raised his eyebrows, but then smiled and said, "Well, I certainly hope you're right. I have had my doubts about the post. But your kind words give me confidence."

Horacio and Mariana took leave of the young imam and continued on their way home. As they walked through the market district, Mariana looked at her husband and held his hand. "I could tell you had an inspiration by the way you became so enthusiastic to hear the imam speak of Zeila."

Horacio nodded. "When I heard what the young cleric said about Zeila, it confirmed my original vision of the book ending up there. That's why I had asked Alessandra to stop in Zeila on her way home to deposit the book in a mosque archive. But not only did the young cleric's words confirm my decision to have Alessandra deposit the book there. It created a new future for the book. One in which the book will end up in Hawaii and be discovered by the very group that I was a part of."

"Hawaii? But don't you think the chances are slim that it might travel from an obscure city on the north coast of Somalia to an obscure island in the Pacific Ocean? Surely you have a stronger reason than this vision or whatever it is."

Horacio puffed up his chest and said in his most magisterial manner, "You forget that I was an academic historian in my earlier life, whose specialty was the Middle East. Or maybe you just like to hear me speak of the book's foreordained path forward." Mariana laughed out loud but then stifled it before anyone would notice. The noon-prayer worshippers were still coming out of the mosque.

Horacio said, "Let's keep walking while I deliver my lecture." He resumed his professorial demeanor. "Here's the connection that appeared in my so-called vision or whatever it was. In the history of Somalia that I studied—which might not happen in this parallel past—Zeila was the city where Ahmad Grañ, the notorious Muslim warrior, would begin his campaign to defeat the Abyssinian emperor, but would be killed before accomplishing his goal. I now believe— strongly believe—that he will be the first person to unwittingly set in motion my book's peregrinations across the globe. When I heard the imam say the name Zeila I saw in my mind Grañ paying a visit to that mosque and taking the mysterious book away with him. My vision went even further. The book would have his nickname, `Left-Handed', embossed on the cover in two languages—Arabic and Amharic." Horacio's pupils became larger, but then he said, "After that, my crystal ball is dark."

Mariana sighed, "But your book does describe the modification. At least the way it's written now. Your instructions to Alessandra were that she should deposit the book in a mosque in Zeila, on the assumption that it would remain there permanently. You said nothing to her about removing the instructions for modifying the astrolabe.

Nor does the book have a cover with those two words embossed on it."

"When I sat down and began writing the book more than 20 years ago, I had just arrived, we hadn't married yet, and Alessandra hadn't been born. I had no expectation that the book would find its way back to the future. I was merely writing a memoir, with all the details, to remind me of what I had gone through. Then, as she was growing up, I was so busy with my work and teaching, I had no time to pick up the book again. When she went away to Italy, the only reason I entrusted the book to her was to have her deposit the book in the Zeila archive. I had assumed the book would remain there forever. But now, after my vision of Grañ taking the book and starting it on its journey, I realize I have to edit the book.

"My plan is to make the necessary changes to the book when she comes home in five years. At that time, there will be ample opportunity to edit out the instructions for converting the astrolabe into a time machine. Then she can make the trip to Zeila and try to have it placed in the mosque archive to await the arrival of Grañ."

"But explain to me why it's necessary that she give the astrolabe to Vasco da Gama. I mean, if this machine is so potentially dangerous— because it might be repaired and be reborn as a time machine—then why not just destroy it? Why give it to anyone?"

"The reason is this. The spherical astrolabe is the only means by which Vasco da Gama and his fleet will survive the return voyage home. They will find that rounding the Cape of Good Hope from west to east to be dangerous, extremely dangerous, and the fleet will barely make it. But the return voyage will be much more dangerous because of the direction of the winds and currents. Being able to use a spherical astrolabe to navigate a safe course will save his fleet."

"But why is it desirable that Vasco da Gama return safely home to Portugal? Wouldn't it be better for the fleet to be destroyed? After all, you've often said that, historically, Portugal's exploration and discovery of the ocean route to India led to widespread destruction and enslavement."

"It's all relative, my dear. Portugal has many would-be navigators eager to try their hand at exploring and establishing the ocean route to India. If Vasco da Gama were to fail to return, it is highly likely that subsequent explorers would be successful, and with much worse outcomes."

"So, what you're saying is that we must enable the lesser of two evils to prevail?"

"Exactly. Da Gama will have established several treaties with East African kingdoms, more or less peacefully and with less cruelty than any possible successor expedition might accomplish. He will go on to complete more voyages to India successfully and will prevent the Spanish, to name just one example, from brutally colonizing the Indies as they will do to the Americas.

"And in the meantime, our brilliant daughter will be able to use the astrolabe in her studies of astronomy, ensuring her success at the University."

A Letter from Home

Alessandra put down her notebook and tried to stop her tears. She had been sitting in an empty classroom at the University of Padua. Neither her professor nor her fellow students had arrived yet for class. She had been attending classes for more than two months and had yet to receive a letter from home. She was worried that something had happened to her parents. She was hungry for the companionship of her parents, even if only in a letter. When her professor entered the classroom and began arranging his lecture materials at the podium, she approached him and asked, "Excuse me professor. I was wondering if there has been some kind of interruption in the mails or other traffic across the Mediterranean."

"Yes, I should say so. The Ottomans have gone crazy, attacking ships all throughout the Eastern Mediterranean. I hear they've begun invading countries, such as Greece and Italy. Nobody has received any letters or packages, or indeed shipments of goods."

Alessandra was stricken with anxiety. She could only hope that the warfare would end soon, and not just because of its effect on the mail. The lingering effects of the Bubonic Plague from the last century had been bad enough. Now warfare was added to society's misery.

As other students began entering the classroom, Alessandra returned to here and now, just another student at the University of Padua. Actually, she was more than just another student. In the space of two months Alessandra had astounded her teachers in each of the subjects she was studying—Astronomy, Arabic, Portuguese and English. Instruction in Arabic and English was a new endeavor by the University. As her first year began, she asked to be "supervised" by professors who would enlist the assistance of foreign scholars in Padua. In fact, she was already fluent in Arabic and English, but needed to complete the courses in order to satisfy the new degree requirements.

But in the case of Portuguese, she genuinely appreciated the help the University's professors gave her. The Portuguese she learned from her parents and aunt and uncle in Mogadishu suffered from two minor flaws. On the one hand, Alessandra's Portuguese was full of Mogadishu colloquialisms that her mother spoke, rather than the "official" Portuguese spoken by people in Oporto, Portugal. That was because Mariana's family had emigrated from Portugal when she was very young and her parents weren't trained teachers.

The other oddity in Alessandra's Portuguese was from her father. His Portuguese was the 20th century form of "classical" Portuguese he had learned in his undergraduate years at the University of Hawaii; he didn't grow up speaking Portuguese at home. So, Alessandra grew up speaking both the 20th century form her dad spoke and the colloquial form her mom spoke. Nevertheless, she appreciated the opportunity to excel in the Portuguese language as taught by her professors.

Astronomy was the subject in which she had to exercise caution and discretion. She frequently reminded herself that she knew more about the solar system and stars than her professors. The instruction she received from her father and the secondary school elective she took last year was enough to put her far ahead of her fellow students, even of her professors. Copernicus and Galileo had not come on the scene yet. But a few of her professors seemed to suggest—at least to her—that they had doubts about the Church-endorsed theory of the solar system—that the earth was the center of the solar system. Those skeptical professors were inclined to believe what she knew to be true—the condemned "heliocentric" theory that the earth and the other planets revolve around the sun. With those professors Alessandra had to tread a fine line. She wanted to encourage them with her questions, yet she knew she couldn't push the issue. It was for the professors to untangle their reasoning, not her. Nevertheless, her encouragement to the professors and students that they continue developing their ideas was widely appreciated, even among the senior faculty.

CHAPTER SIXTEEN

PRESSURE FROM THE ROYALS

The First Female Professor, 1460-1495

In an astonishing turn of events five years later, her graduation from the University with highest honors seemed to push the faculty into doing something they desperately needed to do even though it was unprecedented—they offered her the opportunity to teach Astronomy, Arabic and English at the University. She knew that the faculty really had no choice if they wanted to expand and improve the University's language program, at least regarding Arabic and English. Those languages were becoming very important in the Mediterranean and Levant. The University was pressured by royal and civic benefactors to begin instruction in them. There was no doubt in Alessandra's mind that the University wished to hire her to teach those languages because of that pressure. As for Portuguese, even though there were already several qualified Portuguese scholars on the faculty, they were getting on in years and the University knew it would soon be necessary to hire their replacements.

At first, Alessandra was conflicted. She hadn't intended to stay in Padua beyond graduation; she had planned to return to Mogadishu and join her parents, her aunt and uncle, and her cousin Beatriz in managing the inn. She was especially conflicted because she hadn't received *any* mail from Mogadishu during those five years. But ultimately, she decided to accept the University's offer. And after a year, she was grateful she was given the opportunity to teach. Because of the expansion of the Republic of Venice's influence in the Mediterranean and beyond, the foreign language faculty, and the "Aristotelian" School as a whole, gave Alessandra a lot of support.

Her teaching load left little time for recreation during the school year. Nor was she able to cultivate many friendships among the faculty. But during the summers she took advantage of the two-month break from teaching and writing. Padua was fairly close to other cities and towns in the Veneto. She enjoyed going to Venice on sightseeing and shopping excursions. Another of her favorite destinations was Verona. She rarely ventured to other cities in the regions, mostly because of friction between Venice, Milan and Austria. But she found the time she spent exploring Verona and Venice quite enjoyable.

On Her Own

The University received seven years of mail suddenly during an apparent lull in the fighting in the Mediterranean. But the only letter she received then was a letter from her parish priest, Father Rodrigo. She learned that her father had died only a few years after Alessandra joined the faculty at Padua. She often reread Father Rodrigo's letter:

March 1, 1462

"My dearest Alessandra. I hope you're well up there in Europe. Your father and mother always regretted not being able to visit you there. And now your father will never make that trip, nor will he ever see you again except in the next life. It pains me to have to tell you this, but your father has passed away. I don't know if you noticed in those weeks before you left for Padua, but he was short of breath and even short walks caused such fatigue that he had to rest for several hours.

"His heart finally gave out just a few days ago, on his 94th birthday. I know that Professor Horacio Aleixandre Fuente lived a full life. He was a brilliant scholar and professor, and a loving husband and father.

"I have arranged to have his funeral and burial take place in the cemetery of our *Santo Condestável* Church. That was his wish, and the Church's governing board was very accommodating. I am sure his burial crypt will move you when you finally return home. We had the crypt constructed of brilliant white Carrera marble with light blue veining. I pray you will be able to see your mother again, but her health is rapidly declining. If she passes before your return home, you will see her with your father in their 'Fuente-Mendes Family Crypt.' I am told the crypt will endure for many hundreds of years.

"Well, I must be off to attend to details regarding the burial. May God protect you and assist you in the career you have been blessed with.

"Father Rodrigo."

Not quite two years later, Alessandra received another letter from Father Rodrigo, gently informing her of her mother's passing. She was 82 years old, and according to Father Rodrigo died peacefully in her sleep.

Alessandra's Last Lecture

Alessandra was going over her notes for the lecture she was to deliver in Krakow in two months. She still saw flaws in it; more precisely, concerns. The subject matter—astronomy—wouldn't get her in trouble, but it might get a future student in trouble. Still, she had to be careful in her astronomy lectures and publications, careful not to explicitly endorse a heliocentric theory of the solar system. When she first wrote to her parents 35 years ago to tell them of her concerns, she laughed when she remembered what her father used to tell her about those concerns: "Don't be such a worrywart. Be brave." "Worrywart" was a common term in her father's time, the 20th and 21st centuries, 500 years after Alessandra's time. So, she became brave, even if not outspoken. She knew the ecclesiastical and civil authorities posed no threat, at least not to her. It would happen later to other people.

She tried not to think about the upcoming trip to Krakow, how difficult the road would be. Instead, she looked forward to her retirement. *In less than a year, I'll be free!* She found it hard to believe that she had taught at the University of Padua since she was 25 years old. Astronomy, at least as it was currently taught in Padua, was the least troublesome of those three subjects. "Arabic? How did you come to know Arabic?" she remembered her colleagues asking.

She had been hired when the University had only been in its current form for 66 years. In 1399 it was divided into two schools. The faculty in the "Universitas Iuristarum" taught civil law and Canon law. The "Universitas Artistarum," which had hired Alessandra, offered a wider range of subjects—astronomy, dialectic, philosophy, languages, medicine, and rhetoric.

She smiled as she recalled the reaction of the faculty. She thought she had explained her background well enough to the Masters who governed her School—"I was taught many subjects by private tutors in Mogadishu, including the subjects I propose to teach here at this prestigious University," she had explained. She knew that the University's decision to hire her was based on more than intrigue by her exotic background. She was hired on the strength of her mastery of those subjects, as she demonstrated so well in her grueling three-day examinations. She chuckled as she recalled her examination in Arabic by a resident Arab wholesale merchant originally from Syria. The man was so overjoyed to hear someone—a woman, no less—speak to him in beautiful, classical Arabic, that he wanted to extend the conversation beyond the time allotted for the examination.

But she was pretty sure there were many of her colleagues who found her background not just exotic but suspect. "Mogadishu?

Where is that? Africa? How could that be," she imagined her colleagues asking. Perhaps even more incredible than that was her thorough mastery of English and her ability to teach it to her students, students who came from all over Italy but had never met an Englishman.

She brought herself back to the present. *Thirty-five years is enough! Next year I'll have a real job to do.*

But before she could retire, she had classes to teach, research to conduct and papers to write and deliver. Unlike most of her colleagues, Alessandra did not find research and writing a chore. After all, she was raised by a highly unusual set of parents who not only enrolled her in the best schools in Mogadishu, but hired private tutors who taught her the skills of research and written expression. She often thought about her family's unique history. She had recently begun writing a memoir and often read it over:

It was because of my family's support that I was admitted to the University and subsequently hired by the University. My mother, Mariana Orfeo Mendes, and my aunt and uncle, Catarina and Gonçalo Lopes, were ethnically Portuguese. They were immigrants from Portugal itself. My father, Horacio Aleixandre Fuente, was also Portuguese. But he had grown up in radically different circumstances. He had grown up in a place I've always found difficult to pronounce: "Hawaii." Although his ancestors who had settled in Hawaii were Portuguese, Horacio didn't grow up speaking Portuguese, only English, which he taught me. He learned Portuguese and Arabic in college as part of his professional training. When he met Mariana, he had just become stranded in the past. She helped get him established as a tutor and scribe, and they married a few years later.

Those particulars of her family's backgrounds were obviously not something she could share with her friends and colleagues without endangering her career. Not only would they not believe her, they would brand her crazy.

But that wasn't all she couldn't share with anyone. She couldn't share her father's actual history as opposed to the "history" he told friends and clients in Mogadishu. When she noticed the time, she donned her professor's robe and left her office to give her afternoon astronomy lecture.

Niccoló Copernico

Alessandra arrived at the University of Krakow after an arduous journey from Padua in the spring of 1495. *I'm 60 years old and too old to be making those trips anymore,* she told herself. She would be in Krakow for a week before returning for her last few weeks of the term. Although she had no more scholarly trips planned before retirement, it was of little comfort. She was nervous. Nervous about one more trip she would have to make in the summer of 1496, a trip much longer than the trip to Krakow she had just completed—to Mogadishu, her birthplace. She wished she could still call it her home as well, but she went away to university when she was 20 and was unable to return, not even to visit her parents before they passed.

She had prepared a series of lectures in support of the paper she had published last fall. The reason for her nervousness was her paper's central thesis—an analysis of logical contradictions in the two "official" theories of astronomy—Aristotle's theory of homocentric spheres, and Ptolemy's mechanism of "eccentrics and epicycles." She would use her spherical astrolabe in her lecture on seafaring navigation using the stars as a guide. Alessandra was well aware, based on lessons at the feet of Professor Horacio Fuente that the ideas she would discuss, ever so carefully and ever so respectfully, would not be received well by the Church.

So, it came as a shock when one of the students attending her lectures came up to her and introduced himself as Niccoló Copernico. She hadn't expected to actually meet the great revolutionary thinker and polymath. Of course, when he introduced himself, he was 22 and hadn't yet gone on to greatness. But he was an insightful third-year student at the University of Krakow.

"Professor, you seem to be critical of the accepted theories of Aristotle and Ptolemy. Do I understand you correctly?"

She paused for almost a minute, pretending to gather her papers in preparation for leaving the lecture hall for the morning. Then she sighed, smiled, and said, "Well, Master Copernico, I must say you credit me with too much gall, or foresight, your choice."

"But which is it," he asked with a smile, "gall or foresight?"

"Perhaps the best place to examine these concepts and theories would be somewhere out of the public eye. How about along the banks of the Vistula River? Tomorrow morning's lecture is my final one and then I return to Padua. If we manage to hammer out some clarity on this topic, perhaps I'll use it in a future lecture." And then, with a smile and a wink, she added, "Perhaps you will someday explore the solar system yourself."

For the rest of that morning, and well into her afternoon lecture, Alessandra tried to come up with an answer that would not give away too much, but yet would satisfy this inquisitive young man.

Niccoló attended her lecture the next morning and waited for her to emerge from the hall. They walked to the Vistula, sat down on a grassy rise not too far from the river's bank, and resumed their conversation.

Niccoló said, "I find your lectures interesting, and consistent with some ideas I've had recently."

"Oh really, and what are those ideas of yours?"

"I've been developing the hypothesis that the planets and the sun do not revolve around the earth—that the earth is not the center of the solar system, despite what our benighted priests insist. Indeed, the spherical astrolabe you used in your lecture seemed to at least implicitly endorse the heliocentric theory, that the planets revolve around the sun."

Alessandra looked around to see if anyone was within earshot, and then said, "You must be careful speaking of the Church in that way. I confess I took a risk in using my spherical astrolabe, even though

I used it in the concept of maritime navigation. But I do agree with you. And I think you should expand on your theory; some of my lectures come very close to embracing that theory."

Niccoló sighed. Then he smiled and said, "I'm relieved to hear you say that. I certainly do intend to pursue this idea further."

"I hope you do, Master Copernico." Then, forgetting what she had learned about the historical "Copernicus" from her father, she asked, "Will you graduate this term?"

"No, I've decided to leave university, at least for a while. Family pressures and obligations have made it impossible to continue here for now."

His comment jogged Alessandra's memory. She said, "Well, I have a feeling that whatever you decide to do will be the right choice. But please be careful."

"Thank you. I'm confident that I'm right."

"You are right. Don't be discouraged by any opposition you encounter. I know you'll prevail and show the world."

Her comment surprised him. "I'm somehow encouraged by what you say. I guess I needed someone to tell me I'm not crazy or a heretic. I never expected to get such encouragement from so eminent a scholar as yourself."

With that, they both began walking back to the university. "Well, my faculty apartment is here, so I'll be saying goodbye. My coach will collect me early tomorrow morning. Good luck, and don't give up."

"I won't, you can believe that. Thank you for taking time to talk to me."

On Her Way Home

The trip back to Padua was uneventful, and so was the rest of her time there. Her faculty colleagues seemed genuinely sorry that she could not continue to teach at the University. As her last year at the University was drawing to a close, the head of her School, Professor

Piero Puliti, approached her after a lecture and said, "I must say, Professor Fuente, that I was one of the skeptics who doubted you belonged here. But after I learned of the results of your examinations in astronomy, Portuguese, Arabic and English, I was astounded. As I observed your progress here as the first female professor, I gained new respect for women who have managed to succeed in a man's world."

"Thank you, Doctor Puliti. You do me a great honor, and I will be forever grateful to you."

"Well, before I let you go, will you answer a few questions I have grappled with over the years?"

"Certainly, as well as I am able."

"I can understand how you came to learn Arabic, growing up in Mogadishu. And astronomy and other sciences, I know that many men have studied and advanced those subjects. But how is it that you learned English? I know little of Mogadishu, but from what I've learned, there are no native speakers of that language there."

"Oh, but there are. Or were, until my father died."

"I'm so sorry to hear that. Would you mind telling me a little about your father?"

Alessandra paused so she could recall the story she'd come up with all those years ago and told occasionally in her first year of teaching at the University. "My father, Horacio Fuente, was an inquisitive boy growing up in Oporto. You may remember that Oporto is teeming with foreigners of all nationalities, including merchants and sailors from England and Italy. My father insisted on learning those languages so he could converse with foreigners. He told me he was always interested in traveling and hoped one day to visit Italy and England. His parents both spoke some English and Italian, but haltingly and with a very limited vocabulary. My father wanted to go to university eventually and he knew he would have to pass exams in many subjects. He convinced his parents to hire private tutors."

Professor Puliti nodded, then paused before saying, "That's a wonderful story. Now, back to the subject of astronomy. One of my professional acquaintances at the University of Krakow wrote me not long after your presentations there last year. He seemed to think your lectures might lead some of the students to question the wisdom of the ancients."

"Yes, in fact one of those students came up to me and suggested that very thing. But I set him straight. I explained that my intention was to give an overview of past and current thinking on astronomy."

"That's what my colleague said, but he seemed to be worried about what the Church might think. Were you worried about that?"

"Not at all, Professor. Some who study the ancients, and some who study those who study the ancients, are quite careful to avoid a direct provocation."

Professor Puliti smiled and said, "Some scholars are very careful. I hope you are of that persuasion. Well, I must be off. I wish you the best of luck in your travels. I understand you intend to return to Mogadishu, is that correct?"

"Yes, and I worry about the length and difficulty of the trip—Adriatic Sea, Mediterranean, Red Sea and Indian Ocean. But think it likely the caravels will have improved greatly in the 40 years since I left."

"Oh yes, they have. I have some acquaintances who own caravels. One, a very dear friend, operates two that transport goods up and down the Adriatic. And occasionally he takes on passengers."

Alessandra's eyes widened and she smiled as she said, "I wonder if your friend would consider taking me on as a passenger."

"As I said, he does take passengers on occasion. He has even crossed the Mediterranean in his ship. He has trade agreements with several mercantile houses in Alexandria."

Alessandra exclaimed, "That's my first destination! Do you know anything about the conditions on board his caravels? Would a lady be safe, not to mention comfortable?"

"I am familiar with his ships. I was a passenger on one of them as far down as Bari and back up. The Adriatic is a very calm sea. I don't have personal experience of sailing the Mediterranean, but I have heard the waters can be rough at times. And I would not characterize a passenger's life on a caravel as comfortable."

"May I ask you to inquire of your friend if I might book passage as far as Alexandria?"

"Of course. I was planning on paying him a visit in Venice as soon as my work here at the University is completed for the time being. I'll be going there in a week."

"Thank you so much. My baggage wouldn't amount to much. A trunk of clothes and a trunk for my books and my spherical astrolabe."

"Ah, the spherical astrolabe. I must say, Professor, you amaze me more and more as I talk to you. I almost forgot to ask you about that device, or machine, whatever it is. I understand you have used the spherical astrolabe in your lectures here and at the University of Krakow. What did you demonstrate with it?"

"Seafaring folk have used traditional astrolabes in navigation for centuries. The Portuguese are beginning to use a more advanced device, the spherical astrolabe. My astronomy lectures would be deadly dull without a demonstration of how the modern mariners travel by the stars."

Professor Puliti stopped himself from pursuing the subject in more depth. He moved on to safer waters. "Do you still have family in Mogadishu? You said your parents had passed on."

"Well my parents and my aunt and uncle have passed on, but I still have my cousin and a few friends. I expect to see some of them after I get settled. I'm looking forward to reacquainting myself with the city."

"Well, as I said, or wish I had said, God be with you."

On her last day on campus, the faculty gave her a warm farewell. In the week before, she had begun to make preparations for her long, difficult and uncomfortable trip back "home" to Mogadishu. Except that she was not going all the way to Mogadishu at first. She planned to sail down the Red Sea in a caravel to a city on the Gulf of Aden that Somalis and Arabs call Zeila, near Djibouti. There, she would locate the city's main mosque and arrange to have her father's book stored safely.

Once she completed that task, her next task would be to travel on to Mogadishu and wait for the arrival of the great—some would say infamous—Portuguese explorer, Vasco da Gama. Just as important as securing the safety of the book was seeing that her father's spherical astrolabe—the machine that had brought her father back in time—was offered to the great mariner.

Alessandra's father had repeatedly emphasized the importance of those two tasks; first, finding in Zeila a secure home for his book. She was to arrange to have the book stored in the city's central mosque. The second task will be proceeding to Mogadishu to await the arrival of Vasco da Gama. She had committed her father's explanation of those tasks to memory and occasionally tested herself to make sure she remembered them. Eventually, fearing she might someday forget important details, she committed her memory to paper.

Her father often explained Vasco da Gama's contributions to history and why he would be eager to obtain a better marine navigational tool than the more primitive astrolabes. "You mustn't say anything to da Gama about the broken silver wire on your astrolabe. He will not notice that it's broken because it's inside the small golden globe. The astrolabe's utility as a marine navigational device was not affected by the broken wire. Tell him that the wires are merely decorative and have no function."

She hoped that da Gama would believe her explanation and accept the astrolabe. Even if he noticed the silver wire was broken and attempted to reattach it, he would fail; the tools and materials of the time were inadequate.

Alessandra was fascinated by the history lessons her father taught her as she was growing up. One subject he loved to talk about was the rise to power of the great Somali warrior Ahmad Grañ in 1520. He was born near Zeila, the city Alessandra would visit on her way home and deposit her father's book. Her father explained how momentous Grañ's last campaign against the Abyssinians was—it was the campaign in which he would be killed before he could achieve a victory that would have transformed the socio-political landscape of the Horn of Africa.

Alessandra looked forward to her homeward journey. As she had traveled from Mogadishu to Padua, she would make the journey home by sea—down the Adriatic, across the Mediterranean to Alexandria, by coach to Cairo, another coach to the Port of Suez, and down the Red Sea to Zeila. She did not know how she would keep the book and the spherical astrolabe safe. She prayed that she would succeed.

CHAPTER SEVENTEEN

DEPARTURE FROM PADUA, 1496-1497

Professor Puliti found Alessandra writing in the library where she often had worked on her lectures. "I have good news. My friend tells me he has room on the larger of his two caravels for three passengers. Two of them have already agreed to go. I've taken the liberty of asking him to reserve the third passenger cabin for you."

Alessandra put down her writing materials and said, "Well, that's wonderful news! Yes, I am ready to leave whenever the captain says."

"He tells me he anticipates being finished loading his cargo in two days, and the two other passengers have already arrived and are staying at a nearby inn until the caravel is ready to depart."

"As I said, I am ready to leave. I can gather my trunks and have them ready in front of the library. I will have a student fetch me a carriage."

"That's not necessary. I will have my driver take you in my carriage."

The two-hour trip from Padua to Venice was very comfortable, an unexpected pleasure. Alessandra felt like royalty since she was the only passenger and the carriage was luxurious. The coachman took her directly to the seaport. He directed her to a nearby inn, which he assured her was one meeting the high standards of his master. Alessandra thanked him and signaled for a boy with a cart to load her trunks and take her to the inn. She paid him extra to carry her trunks upstairs to the room she had chosen. She changed into fresh clothes and went downstairs to the common room to get something to eat.

As Alessandra surveyed the room looking for a quiet table, a young gentleman arose from a table at the back of the room and approached her. He was very tall, which made him look thin. There was a look of anticipation mixed with concern in his face. "I hope I'm not being too presumptuous, but I recognized you when you entered the inn. Professor Fuente, my name is Furio Favetti. I was one of your students five years ago."

She was surprised and her face expressed it. "Yes, as a matter of fact you look familiar, but I'm sorry to say I don't remember where I've met you."

"I understand. I was one of the quiet students who didn't engage much with faculty members. I attended your Arabic classes and English classes."

"Bravo. I hope you were satisfied with my teaching. What brings you to Venice?"

"An act of bravery on my part, or perhaps foolishness. Would you care to join me at my table? It's comfortable and out of the way of the door."

As the two of them walked to Favetti's table, Alessandra remarked at the character of the room, with its blonde woods, stained glass lanterns and large square tables of some exotic wood. "I don't believe I've ever seen a common room like this in Padua or, indeed, anywhere else in my travels."

Favetti pulled out a chair from his table and motioned for Alessandra to have a seat. He sat opposite her and motioned to the man behind the bar. Turning to Alessandra he asked, "Would you care for something to eat and drink?"

As the innkeeper approached, Alessandra said, "Yes, I think I'll order something." She said to the man, a distinguished-looking man in late middle age, "You have a very nice establishment. My room upstairs is quite nice." With a smile, she added, "And I'm quite sure the food and drink are reasonably priced and of the highest quality."

The gentleman chuckled and said, "Well, I can assure you the food and ale are excellent. As for the prices, you will be the judge."

After ordering their food and ale, Alessandra smiled and turned to Favetti, "So, tell me, Mr. Favetti, what brings you to Venice?"

"I have signed on as a passenger on the caravel *Sant'Angelo*. I'll be traveling all the way to Alexandria."

"Well, Mr. Favetti, it looks like we will be companions for eight or nine days. I also am bound for Alexandria. What will you be doing in Alexandria?"

Before he could answer, a server came out of the kitchen and delivered their food. The innkeeper brought them a pitcher of ale and two mugs. After the food and drink were arranged on the table, Favetti said, "I represent Mr. William Caxton, a publisher in Bruge who wishes to open a retail establishment in Alexandria offering the latest examples of book publishing. I'm bringing a crate of his books to get started, and in time we hope to have a reliable shipping arrangement established. In addition to those duties, I will translate several titles from English to Italian, which many residents of Alexandria speak. And what about you? Is Alexandria your final destination?"

"Unfortunately, no. I must go further—to Cairo and then to the Port of Suez and down the Red Sea."

Favetti set down his mug and said, "The Red Sea! Whatever for? I know nothing about it except there is very little in the way of civilization in the region."

Alessandra set down her fork and smiled. "Indeed, you know very little about it. In the Arabic classes I taught you, do you not remember my discussion of Mogadishu?"

"Pardon my indiscretion, but now that you have said the name Mogadishu, I do remember you describing it as a hub of commerce with India, China and Persia. What will you do there?"

"I have some business to attend to, and I will probably remain there afterwards for some time. I might end up settling there, after all I was born and grew up there."

For a few minutes the two of them turned their attention to their food. Before they could resume their conversation, a pudgy young man who looked to be about 18 approached. "Pardon my interruption, but I overheard you talking about traveling on the *Sant'Angelo* when she sails next. I also have booked passage on that worthy craft. All the way to Alexandria, which I overheard you saying is your destination as well."

Alessandra smiled, turned to Favetti and said, "It seems we must be more discrete." Turning back to the young man standing near them, she said, "Kind sir, won't you please have a seat with us. And tell us about yourself."

The young man took a seat across the table from them and said, "My name is Marco Caratto. I am apprenticed to Master Angelo Barovier, the preeminent glassblowing artist of Murano. I am in my fourth year, and he has entrusted me with a quantity of his glass artistry to sell to the Alexandria merchants of fine art."

Favetti said, "I have heard of him. I'm certain his fame will soon spread throughout the region. But please, if you will, have a meal with us."

Alessandra signaled to the innkeeper and when he came to their table, Marco said, "I'll just have a plate of the local catch if it's fresh, kind sir. And a small ale."

The innkeeper smiled. "As you wish, young master. I do hope the fish meets your approval."

Marco smiled sheepishly and said, "Forgive me. I'm sure it's fresh. I had some last evening at an inn not far from here and I couldn't eat it."

The evening passed pleasantly as the three travelers shared stories of their work and hopes for the future. Alessandra retired to her room looking forward to the journey.

The next morning the three of them met again for an early meal before the time came for them to make their way to the port. As they were eating and talking, a messenger entered the inn and, seeing the three of them at table, approached and told them the caravel was in the final stage of loading and would be ready to depart before noon.

The innkeeper overheard and approached. "If you wish I will summon a carriage. They are very speedy and will deliver you to the port in time."

The Caravel Sant'Angelo

The captain of the caravel, a middle-aged man of Slavic appearance, introduced himself and welcomed them as the three passengers presented themselves at the shipping office. "I am Captain Pavel Novak. I believe my ship will be ready to depart in an hour. Please follow me and I will show you to your cabins." The captain led them onto the ship's main deck. He pointed to the Master's Cabin and then to the Wardroom, explaining that meals for officers and passengers would be served there. Pointing to a set of descending stairs he said, "Those lead to the lower deck and the three cabins where you'll be sleeping. There won't be room in them for your trunks, which will be stowed below in the Lower Hold. But before you have them taken below you may take out the items you think you'll need on the voyage. Of course, you will have access to the trunks, which will be quite secure. I anticipate our trip to Bari will take two days. We will take on supplies, offload cargo, and take on other cargo. That will probably require a day. Then we will depart for Alexandria, a trip of about six days."

The captain was not exaggerating when he said the cabins were small. Alessandra found that her small case of a weeks' worth of simple clothing and personal items barely fit at the foot of the small cot. There was a small sink with a basin and pitcher, and a chamber pot under her cot. Stretched across the cot was a thin mattress on a piece of canvas. Alessandra pulled back the coverlet to inspect the sheet. It appeared to be clean. She lay down on the bed to feel how comfortable, or uncomfortable, it was. "This will do," she murmured as she began to drift off to sleep.

Sleep didn't quite arrive, however. She was startled by a knock on the door. Opening it she was greeted by Furio. "I have been informed that the captain and officers will take the evening meal in an hour, and we have been invited to join them."

"That's wonderful. I haven't eaten much today. I will join you there."

Sitting at the rectangular table were Captain Novak and two ship's officers, Dalmatin and Brenner. Alessandra, Marco and Furio joined them. First Mate Dalmatin, a handsome young man from Croatia, said to Alessandra, "You are not the first female passenger we have taken aboard the *Sant'Angelo*, even all the way to Alexandria. If I may be so bold, what is the purpose of your trip?"

Feeling a bit out of place on board the ship, Alessandra said, "I am aware that it is uncommon for a female to book passage on sea-going ships. But this is not my first trip on the Adriatic, or indeed across the Mediterranean. My purpose is to return to the home of my youth."

Captain Novak smiled and said to his two officers, "My friend Professor Puliti in Padua tells me that Miss Fuente has just retired as Professor of Astronomy and Languages." Turning to Alessandra he said, "I find it very interesting, if not astonishing, that you are traveling beyond Alexandria, down the Red Sea in fact. Mogadishu, is it?"

"Yes, that's correct. I was born in Mogadishu to Portuguese parents and left when I was 20 to attend the University of Padua, followed by my academic career five years later. I retired not long ago and am returning home."

Chief Engineer Brenner, an older man with a classic Nordic appearance, asked, "What languages did you teach?"

"I taught Arabic, Portuguese and English. I was the first female member of the faculty. Perhaps my proficiency in those subjects was the reason I was offered the position; they had no one else and there was a growing interest in those languages."

Novak asked Caratto and Favetti to enlighten him and his officers as to their purpose on this trip. Favetti said, "Captain Novak, the crate I am bringing with me is filled with books, the most modern type of book, printed and bound by Mr. William Caxton of Bruge. I will be his agent in Alexandria."

Caratto said, "And I will be arranging for my crate of artistic Murano glassware to be sold to Alexandria merchants."

There was a period of silence as the group began eating. From time to time, a cook's helper entered the room to deliver more food and wine. Brenner asked Alessandra, "I once lived for a time in Alexandria and heard stories of Mogadishu. It is quite an amazing city by all accounts. I heard one story, don't know if it's true, that a Chinese Admiral once arrived at the city with a fleet of huge `treasure ships,' as the story goes."

Alessandra paused before answering, mostly to control a feeling of sadness that was threatening to show on her face. "Your story is quite true, Mr. Brenner. That fleet arrived well before I was born. But I heard many stories of the Chinese sailors and merchants who entered the city in great numbers, buying and selling large quantities of goods."

First Mate Dalmatin asked, "Your name suggests you are Portuguese. I didn't know there were Portuguese in Mogadishu."

"There are many different groups in Mogadishu, Europeans, Arabs, Persians, Chinese and Africans. My parents were Portuguese immigrants from Oporto."

"So, they emigrated from Oporto together?" Dalmatin asked.

"No, they did not know each other in Oporto. Their parents brought them to Mogadishu as children."

Captain Novak asked, "My friend Professor Puliti told me you learned English in Mogadishu. Were there many English speakers there?"

"Not many at all. My father had learned some of the language as a child in Oporto and insisted I learn it growing up. He believed it was becoming an important language to learn. He engaged tutors for me in English, history, astronomy, mathematics and other sciences."

"Ah, astronomy." Captain Novak exclaimed. "Now that's an important subject these days of maritime travel. I understand the Arabs and Portuguese were excellent mariners and depended on their charts and astrolabes to keep them from getting lost."

Alessandra didn't want to delve into the subject of astrolabes for fear of betraying too much knowledge of the subject. "Yes, that's true. The oceans are becoming more and more dominated by the Portuguese, English and Spanish."

"Professor Puliti told me you used a type of astrolabe in your astronomy classes, a spherical astrolabe, the most advanced type. I understand you are bringing the astrolabe back home with you."

"Yes, that's correct. It's a family heirloom, you might say."

Captain Novak pushed his plates back and stood. "Well, it's time for the First Mate and Chief Engineer to get back to work on the main deck, and for me to resume going over my paperwork in my office. This has been a most enjoyable conversation, and I hope we'll continue it as the days go by."

Alessandra said, "Oh, Captain Novak. I have one request of you. Would you escort me down into the lower hold? I would like to see where my trunks are located if I should need to retrieve something."

The Captain agreed and escorted Alessandra to the stairs leading down to the lower hold. "I'll leave you here. You may need to move something to get access to your trunks. Ask one of the sailors down there to assist you if necessary."

Alessandra was relieved to see that boxes and crates surrounded her trunks. Doubting that she would need anything from it for the duration, she ascended the stairs and went to her cabin.

For the next two days Alessandra spent most of her time out on the main deck enjoying the sea air and reading. There were several pens containing farm animals, but most cargo was stowed in the lower hold. She occasionally chatted with her two companions, but the sailors were too busy to engage in conversation. Meals were in the Wardroom as before. The Adriatic was calm, the weather was clear, and there was no turbulence. Each evening after supper she would check on her trunks and was relieved that nothing had changed.

At Bari events took place as Captain Novak had described. The *Sant'Angelo* docked an hour before noon, spent the daylight hours tied up while cargo was unloaded and new cargo loaded. Alessandra watched the process, both out of an abundance of caution and curiosity. The crew was experienced and efficient. By nightfall, they left port. Before dawn the next day they passed Otranto and began the crossing of the Mediterranean.

The sea was calm and voyage unremarkable until two days later as they approached Crete from the west. They encountered several mild storms, mercifully short. The ship then began sailing in a southeasterly direction. The next four days were tedious but blessedly free of adventure.

Alexandria

The *Sant'Angelo* reached the Port of Alexandria early in the morning. Captain Novak saw that his passengers' possessions were safely offloaded and placed in a secure enclosure in the Port warehouse. "Milady and young lords, your belongings will be safe here temporarily until you are able to have them transported to their final destination in the city."

The Captain sent a runner to hail a carriage to take them into the city. As they waited for the carriage, Alessandra said, "Before I take leave of you, I must warn you of two things. First, as you will discover, Alexandria is little more than a garrison town of some 8,000 souls. Its primary purpose is to enable the Mamluk governor of Egypt to prevent any invading Ottoman force from entering Egypt. Second, as you will also discover, Christians are treated very poorly in Egypt, notwithstanding the large population of Coptic Christian Egyptians. Christians, especially Christian merchants, are heavily taxed."

Furio frowned and said, "I was not aware of what you are saying. It would seem that I neglected my studies in history as I focused on learning about the book trade. Why are Christians subject to heavier taxation?"

"Muslim governments everywhere do not trust their Christian citizens to take up arms in defense against invaders. So instead they are taxed in lieu of military service."

Marco seemed agitated. "If, as you imply, Alexandria is not wealthy, it would seem there is little market for expensive Venetian glassware. Wouldn't Cairo itself be a better market not only for Venetian glassware but for books in foreign languages?"

Alessandra paused as she attempted to formulate an answer that would not prompt questions as to the basis of her knowledge. "Certainly, Cairo with its 400,000 souls and a thriving mercantile class would be a much better location for your two business enterprises. I didn't mean to imply that there would be no market for your goods in Alexandria. You will do well enough. But I must warn you. I have studied the history of Ottoman Turkish expansion into Anatolia and the Levant. The Ottomans and Mamluks have long been adversaries. The Ottomans' goal is to control most of the Mediterranean region. I would not be surprised if they attacked Cairo sometime in the next 20 years, or sooner."

When the carriage for Furio and Marco arrived, Alessandra said, "But I do have one suggestion, which I think is a good one. While your goods are still in the warehouse, consider this: a much better location to set up a thriving business would be Istanbul itself. It's a large, prosperous city that is under no danger of attack or decline."

Furio said, "Well, I suggest that Marco and I spend a day or two in Alexandria before we decide what to do." Marco nodded a little nervously.

With that, Alessandra bid the two of them farewell. After their coach left, Alessandra returned to the warehouse to confer with Captain Novak.

CHAPTER EIGHTEEN

THE RED SEA

Alessandra saw that the Captain had just walked away from a group of warehousemen. She signaled to him and said, "Captain Novak, I wonder if you can recommend a safe and inexpensive mode of transport to the Port of Suez."

"Suez! Oh, yes, I forgot you are planning to travel on to Mogadishu. You will have to go to Cairo first. The road is well traveled and safe. Several coaches travel the road every day. From Cairo, there are horse-drawn wagons that travel frequently to the Port of Suez. Some are strictly for transporting goods, some transport goods and passengers, and some transport passengers exclusively. All are covered to protect goods and passengers from the elements."

"That sounds wonderful! I'm so relieved, because when my father brought me up to Alexandria as a 20-year-old girl, we had to travel from Suez to Alexandria in a merchant caravan. And what about down the Red Sea and beyond?"

The Captain smiled and said, "You'll find many types of craft that regularly ply the Red Sea and farther, all the way to Mozambique. There are caravels such as the one that brought you here, and there are the lighter and faster *sambuq* ships that also travel the length of the Red Sea. If I were you, I would choose the *sambuq*, which can make the trip from Suez to Mogadishu in seven days. On the other hand, if you choose a caravel, which would add another day on the trip, you would have a better chance of being taken aboard as a passenger. On either craft you would find the Red Sea and Indian Ocean much calmer than the Mediterranean. And you'll be able to see coral reefs and all manner of fish."

"Thank you, Captain Novak! I'm relieved to hear that such crafts still ply those waters. It was a caravel that transported me from Mogadishu to the Port of Suez when I left to begin my studies and teaching career at Padua. Although the ship was transporting many bales and crates, there were three passenger cabins, and I was one of three lucky passengers to get one. I will be content to book passage on either type of vessel. Although I am not under any time constraints, I would like to spend as little time on a ship as possible."

At Captain Novak's direction, Alessandra's trunks were carted over. She hired the driver to take her the short distance to where the coaches to Cairo assembled. She approached the driver of one coach and found there was room inside for one more passenger. After her trunks were loaded on the open platform at the rear she climbed inside the carriage. There were two other passengers, both of whom appeared to be sailors judging from their clothes. She smiled and said, "Greetings. Where are you coming from?"

The older man said, "We are returning to the sea after a short spell in Alexandria with our families. My name is Aristide and this is my brother Castor."

Alessandra said, "Very pleased to meet you. My name is Alessandra and I'm returning home to Mogadishu."

Aristide looked surprised. "Your home is Mogadishu? I would have thought a lady such as yourself would be from Cairo, not a remote, little-known place like Mogadishu."

Alessandra chuckled, "I often get that reaction when I say my home is Mogadishu. It may be little known to people from Alexandria, as it is to people from Padua, where I worked for more than 30 years. But I can assure you it is neither remote nor little known to the people of East Africa and the Indian Ocean."

Castor asked, "What work did you do in Padua? We have met travelers from Padua on our ship."

"I was professor of astronomy and languages. What is your ship?"

"We're crew members on the *Aurora*, a caravel that travels between the Port of Suez and Aden. Aden is a prosperous city. What is Mogadishu like?"

"It is a very prosperous city almost as large as Cairo. It has grown rich from trade with cities on the African coast, Ceylon, India and China."

Aristide asked, "You said the city was your home. Were you born there? You appear to be European."

"Yes, I was born in Mogadishu but my parents and aunt and uncle were originally from Portugal. They owned an inn in Mogadishu. My father was also a scribe and professor. After my parents and aunt and uncle died, my cousin and I inherited the inn. She has been managing it all these years."

After another hour, the conversation waned and the passengers contented themselves by looking out at the countryside.

By mid-afternoon, the coach arrived in Cairo. Alessandra asked, "May I be so bold as to suggest that we three travel together to the Port of Suez? It would be more comfortable than traveling with strangers."

Aristide laughed, "We are hardly more than strangers ourselves. But yes, your suggestion is a good one. My brother and I know several of the coachmen and we'll find one of them to take us on to Suez."

The road to Suez was barely more than half the distance from Alexandria to Cairo. By the time they arrived, it was early evening. Castor helped Alessandra retrieve her trunks and get them on a cart headed for the pier. "I see a caravel docked next to ours. I believe it's the *Mythos*, a strong, seaworthy craft. Shall we see if the captain is taking passengers?"

"That would be most helpful. I find that acquaintanceship is a strong bond."

When they got to the pier, Aristide said, "I'll take our trunks to the *Aurora*. Castor will introduce you to Captain Negasi Seyoum of the *Mythos*."

Alessandra was in luck. There was one cabin available. She removed her small case from one of the trunks, took out the small cloth bag containing the clothing she had worn on the *Sant'Angelo*, and refilled the case with clean clothes. *I hope I'll be able to wash my dirty laundry on board the ship!*

The ship was due to depart in two hours. Captain Seyoum asked a deckhand to load Alessandra's trunks into the Lower Hold. Seyoum appeared to be in his early 60's. He was very tall, had green eyes, wavy hair, and a light reddish-brown complexion. He spoke to his crewmen with a tone of respect.

Alessandra took leave of Aristide and Castor and boarded the ship. Before going below to her cabin, she stood on the main deck to stretch and take in the salt air.

"I'm pleased to learn you are going to Mogadishu. May I ask what draws you to my city?"

Alessandra flinched. "Oh, Captain, you surprised me. Are you a native of Mogadishu also?"

"Yes, as a matter of fact I am."

"Judging from your name I would guess that you are Abyssinian, or born of Abyssinian parents."

"You are very astute. My family emigrated to Mogadishu from Harar to escape growing tension between Christians and Muslims."

Alessandra found it very easy to talk to the captain. Not wanting the conversation to end she said, "I wonder if our families ever met. My family owned an inn. My father also was a professor and scribe."

Captain Seyoum smiled and nodded. "I lived in Mogadishu for 20 years and then took jobs on the many vessels sailing up and down the Red Sea and Indian Ocean. My mother may well have availed herself of your father's skills. She had to draw up documents showing a legal transfer of ownership of my late father's property. Did your father draft legal documents such as contracts and leases?"

"Yes, many times. He also helped write letters for people."

At this point the Captain could see the First Mate signaling to him. "Well, I see that I am needed on the Quarterdeck. I hope that we can continue our conversation from time to time."

"I look forward to it."

As the Captain walked away, he turned and said, "I'll send someone to your cabin in the morning to invite you to the Wardroom to join me, the officers and the other passengers, for the morning meal."

As she did when she was a passenger on the *Sant'Angelo*, Alessandra went down to the Lower Hold to check to see that her trunks were securely stowed in the midst of other crates. In fact, they were behind several crates. She wondered how difficult it would be to move them to get access to her trunks during the weeklong voyage to Mogadishu.

By the time she was finished inspecting her cabin, she was too tired to attempt conversation with anyone. As she lay in bed on the cusp of sleep, she felt the ship begin moving under sail. *Onward to my home*, she mumbled before sleep overcame her.

The next morning the Captain, First Mate Orozco and Chief Engineer Hassan welcomed the passengers to the table inside the cramped Wardroom. Captain Seyoum introduced himself and asked the passengers if they would like to introduce themselves and the purpose of their trip. Alessandra spoke first, "My name is Alessandra Fuente. I recently retired as Professor of Astronomy and Languages at the University of Padua. I am returning to my home, Mogadishu."

The older of the other passengers said, "My name is Abbasi Kassab. I have accepted the position of Archivist at the *Masjid Fakhr'ad-Din*, the oldest mosque in Mogadishu. It is located in the Hamar Weyne district."

At a nod from Captain Seyoum, the younger man said, "I am Ghanam Shalhoub. I am hoping to establish an import-export business in Mogadishu. My company in Cairo is very successful and I intend to expand into Mogadishu. I have heard many accounts of Mogadishu as a prosperous trading center where ships and caravans arrive weekly."

Alessandra said, "Indeed it is, Mr. Shalhoub. I lived there for 20 years before leaving for the University. Mr. Kassab, you said the *Masjid Fakhr'ad-Din* is the oldest in the city. I would imagine the mosque has a large library."

"Yes, I'm told it is the largest in the region. I'm looking forward to beginning my tenure there."

Alessandra wondered how that mosque compared to those in Zeila.

The Captain said, "Mr. Shalhoub, I am very familiar with the city, having been born and raised there. Perhaps I can recommend some areas of the city you might find suitable for your business."

Alessandra added, "My mother owned a successful inn for many years and had many dealings with business owners in the city. I can give you some information about opportunities during our trip."

Captain Seyoum smiled at Alessandra then said to the group, "I look forward to getting to know you all."

Alessandra waited for everyone to leave the cabin and then asked Seyoum, "Captain, will you be making a port call at Djibouti or Zeila? I have some business in Zeila before I travel on to Mogadishu."

Captain Seyoum looked surprised. "As a matter of fact, we will be making a port call at Zeila shortly after dawn. I told that to the two gentlemen but I neglected to tell you. We have goods to offload and goods to bring on board, not to mention other supplies and water. We will be docked two nights before continuing on to Mogadishu. I'm surprised you would have business there. I thought you were headed home to Mogadishu."

"Yes, Mogadishu is my home. But I must go into Zeila and deliver a package to the *Masjid al-Qiblatayn*, the oldest mosque in the city. I hope I'll be able to complete that task in time to get back to the ship before nightfall."

"I'm certain you will. That mosque is not far from the port."

"Have you spent time in Zeila? I know very little about it."

"Yes, in my early days I captained smaller vessels up the Indian Ocean coast as far as Djibouti. But not since I began captaining caravels. If you like, I can have my chief engineer, Mr. Hassan, take you to the mosque. He was planning to visit the *Suq* anyway to buy ship's supplies."

Alessandra was relieved. "That would be wonderful. Are you sure he won't be needed on board the ship?"

"Well, not for the first few hours when goods are being offloaded."

The remainder of the Red Sea portion of the voyage took almost six days. Alessandra found it very restful and found the Red Sea itself to be fascinating. Captain Seyoum was careful to avoid the many coral reefs, especially those near the western shore. In some areas, Alessandra could see the reefs through the shallow waters. As the *Mythos* passed through the narrow Bab el Mandeb strait, Alessandra could see the African coast clearly. Soon the ship passed the Port of Djibouti.

Captain Seyoum approached Alessandra and said, "We should arrive at Zeila in an hour or so. Would you like me to have your trunks moved so you can retrieve your package?"

"Yes, thank you." Alessandra walked down to the lower hold and watched as a crewman moved boxes and bales away from her trunks. When the trunks were clear, she untied the ropes around the larger trunk. Alessandra opened it and could see that the inside was dry. The various boxes and packages were still as she had arranged them. The box containing the spherical astrolabe was nestled snugly between two boxes of her writing materials. A smaller box next to them contained her father's book and was doubled wrapped in silk fabric and oilcloth. She was relieved to see that the oilcloth was undisturbed. She carefully removed the box, rearranged the trunk's contents to keep things from shifting, closed the trunk and retied the ropes. *Now for the fun part—convincing the mosque imam to allow me to store the book in a secure place!*

Zeila

After the ship docked the chief engineer walked up to Alessandra and smiled. "Shall we venture forth into the city?"

"I'm ready. I have my package. I hope the *Masjid al-Qiblatayn* isn't too far from port."

"It is only a short walk." They walked down the gangplank and began walking into the city. The chief engineer said, "By the way, my name is Ibrahim Hassan. I found your introduction fascinating. I don't believe the *Mythos* has ever had a passenger from Padua. I would love to hear more about the city and the University when we resume our journey to Mogadishu."

"It would be my pleasure. Where are you from, Mr. Hassan?"

"I was born in Begemdir in the Semien Kingdom of Abyssinia, but left to seek opportunities on ships. I have been on Captain Seyoum's caravel for almost 10 years."

"That's interesting. The stories I heard of Abyssinia said nothing about Muslims in that Kingdom, just a period of prolonged battles between the Beta Israel people and the Christian Emperor."

Hassan smiled. "I understand why you assume I am Muslim, because of my name Ibrahim Hassan. But I am Jewish; at least on my mother's side."

"Oh, I'm sorry if I offended you. But how did you end up so far from your home?"

"I had no desire to fight and die in the battles between Beta Israel and the Christian Emperor Yeshaq. So I left my home in 1460 when

I was 20. I lived in Djibouti for about 25 years before I was hired by Captain Seyoum.”

“Do you know anything about Zeila? My father visited it from Mogadishu and told me a little about his trip. But I was young.”

“Well, Zeila has been part of the Adal Sultanate for the past 70 years. The city is home to people from many different lands and is relatively peaceful.”

Alessandra knew from her father that the Sultanate would only last for another 20 years or so, until Ahmad Grañ rose to power. Her father often regaled her and her mother with thrilling, but gruesome, stories of the many battles that he believed would take place before Grañ would be killed. His widow would marry another powerful ruler who would transfer the capital to Harar.

Alessandra and Mr. Hassan walked for a few more minutes when the mosque came into view. Mr. Hassan said, “I must turn here and head off to buy some supplies for the ship at the *Suq*. I can meet you in this spot in an hour or so. If your errand lasts longer than an hour, I believe you know your way back to the ship.”

Mr. Hassan walked away down a busy street and Alessandra continued on to the mosque. Once there she removed her shoes, covered her head with a scarf and washed her feet in the basin by the entrance. When she entered, the beauty of the mosque took her breath away.

It was midmorning and the faithful had not yet assembled for the noon prayers. A very distinguished-looking man came out of a room at the rear of the mosque. When he saw Alessandra, he walked up and greeted her. After they exchanged the formal pleasantries the man introduced himself in Portuguese. "I am Imam Abdullah Assad, the prayer leader of the mosque. I am also the mujtahid for the madrasa behind the mosque and archivist in the large library in the rear there." He chuckled and said, "I wear many hats, as I once heard an Englishman say."

Alessandra answered in Arabic, "I'm very pleased to meet you. My name is Alessandra Fuente."

Imam Abdullah raised his eyebrows. "You speak beautiful Arabic! But your name sounds familiar. You are Portuguese, no?"

"Yes, but I was born and raised in Mogadishu."

"Ah, yes, now I remember where I heard the name Fuente. Many years ago, when I was a junior imam at the *Masjid Faisal* of Mogadishu, I met a charming couple with that name."

Alessandra realized that Imam Abdullah was the young imam her parents wrote her about when she was a brand-new student at the University of Padua. She decided to get right to the point. "Your memory is accurate. In fact, Horacio Fuente and Mariana Mendes were my parents. They were impressed with you and urged me to visit you and your mosque after I retired."

Imam Abdullah took a deep breath and exhaled slowly. "I'm not quite sure what to say, except that I am very pleased to meet you. Your parents gave me a lot of encouragement. I think their praise of Zeila was probably the main reason for my determination to make this mosque truly grand."

"I am so glad to hear that. I would love to learn more about your mosque. Would it be too much to ask you for a tour?"

"Not at all, it would be my pleasure. I love showing off this lovely and impressive institution."

For the next half hour, the Imam led Alessandra through the

mosque, the madrasa, the archive room and the library. As they were standing in the library, Alessandra said, "Imam Abdullah, my father entrusted me with this very book he wrote." Drawing the book out of her girdle purse, she said, "When he met you in Mogadishu, and you told him you would become Imam of the *Masjid al-Qiblatayn* in Zeila, he had a very strong emotional and spiritual reaction. A vision in fact, that this mosque's archive would be a secure home for his book. Might I ask you if you would honor my father's wish and place his memoir in your archive?"

Imam Abdullah looked surprised. "A vision you say. Well, I believe visions can be portents of things to come. That is especially true in this case, because I have long believed that the Adal Sultanate would give way in the future. I just hope and pray that this mosque will survive the turmoil."

"According to my father, his vision foresaw the continued existence of the mosque. If my father's vision is true, you do not have anything to worry about."

"Well, I would be honored to give your father's book a proper home. Shall we go back into the archive? We can decide where your father's memoir belongs."

Once in the archive room Alessandra said, "I see you are taking good care of these documents and books. Even memoirs. Do you think you could keep this with other memoirs?"

"Of course."

Alessandra handed it to him and said "I think it best to keep the book wrapped in the oilcloth. That will protect it from the humidity."

Handling the book carefully the Imam thanked Alessandra and walked to the rear of the room. Along the wall on the left was a head-high shelf on which there were a dozen books bound in red leather embossed with Arabic calligraphy. Imam Abdullah placed Alessandra's book at one end of the shelf, upright and with the cover facing toward the room. Turning back to Alessandra he said, "Do you think this will be a satisfactory location? Your father's book doesn't stand out as much as these other rather garish books."

"I think it will be fine there. I thank you from the bottom of my heart for your kindness."

"It is my pleasure to honor your father's memory in this way. No harm will come to his book here in the archive."

Alessandra thanked the Imam again as she stepped outside the entrance. "Soon I will be returning to my beloved Mogadishu. I hope to pay you a visit after I am settled there."

Alessandra walked out of the mosque and back to the street. Just then she saw Mr. Hassan walking toward her. A man pulling a cart loaded with ship's supplies walked behind him. He nodded and said, "From your expression I would say you had a successful visit with Imam Abdullah."

"Yes, very. Do you know him?"

"I met him last year when he came to the port to greet an important Muslim dignitary on board the ship. The dignitary complimented the captain and officers for the condition of the ship. The Imam smiled and thanked us before escorting his guest to the mosque."

CHAPTER NINETEEN

MOGADISHU, 1497-1499

Home, July 1947

Back on the caravel, Alessandra had a leisurely six days before the ship would reach Mogadishu. When she wasn't sleeping, eating or talking with the Captain, officers and fellow passengers, she did lots of reading. She liked nothing better than to sit on the Main Deck, wedged between bales of cloth and leather, and read. Before the ship departed Zeila, she took reading and writing material from a box in her trunk. The two Arabic books she enjoyed most were two she had purchased before leaving for Padua in 1455. Arab travelers who had visited Mogadishu wrote them. Ibn Battuta traveled extensively throughout Africa and visited Mogadishu in 1332. He described it as "an exceedingly large city" with many rich merchants, a madrasa and a community of descendants of the Prophet. He described the nearby city of Kilwa as having a school of law.

Ibn Khaldun wrote a more recent book in 1400 about Mogadishu, describing the city as a large metropolis that served as the capital of the Ajuran Kingdom. He wrote that Mogadishu had many buildings of three and four stories and many wealthy merchants. Alessandra always chuckled at Ibn Khaldun's description of Somalis as being "nomad in character" despite the size and wealth of the city.

Alessandra's father had told her that Mogadishu's current population was at least 40,000, about the same as Padua's population.

Alessandra and her cousin Beatriz could have written a book about Mogadishu themselves—its evolution, amazing ethnic variety, and status as a major mercantile center on the Indian Ocean. Her father's career as a scribe, notary and translator provided him and the family with many stories of his clients' activities in the city. She had begun to write her memoir of the city.

Toward late afternoon on the last day of July 1497, Mr. Hassan informed the three passengers that the caravel *Mythos* would be coming into the Port of Mogadishu before dark. Alessandra finished writing in her journal and penned a reminder that she had a little over 16 months to prepare to meet Vasco da Gama.

Her father had told her the history of Vasco da Gama's voyages around the tip of Africa, to India, and back to Portugal. Her father said that during his academic career he had read the journals of an unnamed scribe on Vasco da Gama's flagship, the *São Gabriel*, who kept meticulous details of the first voyage. The scribe wrote that on da Gama's return voyage from India he dropped anchor off Mogadishu on the night of January 2, 1499. The fleet did not intend to enter the harbor of Mogadishu. The ships would pass by the harbor the next morning and sail on. The scribe also wrote something that Horacio found intriguing—at dawn on January 2, Vasco da Gama fired several cannon blasts as it raised anchor and sailed on to Malindi.

Alessandra had practically memorized her father's bare-bones explanation of what she would have to do with the spherical astrolabe: "Vasco da Gama knows nothing about the city, never having read the accounts of it written by Ibn Battuta and Ibn Khaldun. He will be in a hurry to get to the destination he is familiar with—Malindi, further south on the coast of East Africa. You will have to find a way to go out to his ship, the *São Gabriel*, and offer him the spherical astrolabe. Perhaps he will fire off his cannons in thanks!"

Captain Seyoum ordered some crewmen to move his three passengers' crates and trunks out onto the dock and asked them what they wished to do with them. Kassab and Shalhoub asked for a carriage to take them and their belongings to any inn the Captain might recommend. He directed them to a nearby carriage stand and recommended an inn.

Then Captain Seyoum turned to Alessandra and asked, "And which inn are you going to?"

"I will ask for a carriage to take me and my trunks to the inn called *Funduq Mendes*. Do you know it?"

Captain Seyoum looked startled at first but then he smiled. "Yes, I do know it. It's very large. I recall you telling me about your parents owning an inn in Mogadishu. Is that the inn that your parents own?"

"It's the inn that my family own with another family: Catarina and Gonçalo Lopes and their daughter Beatriz. My mother was Catarina's sister. Both sets of parents have since passed away. My cousin Beatriz and I are co-owners. She manages the inn now."

"Did the two families name the inn *Funduq Mendes*?"

"Yes, the inn is named after my mother's father, who was the brother of Beatriz's mother. My mother also wanted to honor the great Galician noblewoman, Elvira Mendes. My mother learned about her from her mother, who had learned about her in school. My mother told me about Elvira Mendes's life and her marriage to King Alfonso of Leon. Anyway, I surely hope Beatriz received my letter."

"Well, as you know mail from Europe to Somalia is extremely slow, sometimes taking as long as two months. It generally takes the same route you took—across the Mediterranean, then overland to Cairo and the Port of Suez, and finally down the Red Sea and Indian Ocean coast of southern Somalia. During the sporadic warfare between the Ottomans, the Venetians and the Genoese, commercial shipping of all sorts was interrupted, often permanently."

The Innkeeper of Funduq Mendes

Beatriz and Alessandra had grown up together since the age of two and felt like sisters. Beatriz had been running the *Funduq Mendes* since their parents passed away over 30 years ago. Alessandra had been at the University of Padua more than nine years at that point.

The inn was a very large two-story, horseshoe-shaped building. Before Mariana's father purchased it many years ago, it had been the Sultan's seat of government. But after the Sultan moved his governmental offices closer to the Port, the building had lain dormant for several years. Finally, the Sultan decided to sell it and Mariana's father was the lucky bidder. He immediately began renovating it so he could operate it as an inn.

On the ground floor at the bottom of the "U" was the entrance to the inn, which opened into a large lobby. The reception desk and the office were directly across the lobby from the entrance. On the right side of the lobby were a common room, dining room and kitchen. A doorway in between the office and reception opened to a hallway. The right and left ends of the hallway led to the two-story arms of the "U," each with a short staircase leading to the second floor. The arms of the "U" had three guest rooms on each floor. The arms were over 40 feet long and 10 feet wide. They enclosed a large vegetable garden that was fenced at the top of the "U." Each of the 12 guest rooms had a window looking out onto the enclosed garden on one side and a door to the hallway on the other.

In the middle of the hall behind the reception desk was a door leading upstairs. There were two very large private suites upstairs, each consisting of two bedrooms, a bathroom and a library. Each suite had two windows—one facing the street and one facing the garden. Before Mariana and Horacio passed away, they lived in the suite on the right with Alessandra. Beatriz, Catarina and Gonçalo lived in the suite on the left. The two couples owned the inn jointly, and everyone participated in the running of the inn.

Beatriz heard the front door open and then footsteps coming toward the office. She put down the inn's financial ledger book, stood up from her desk and walked out of the office. Her face lit up when she saw who had just entered the inn. "Am I glad to see you, my beloved cousin, Alessandra Fuente!!"

The two women laughed as they hugged each other.

"And I as well, dear, dear Beatriz! I hope life has treated you well and fairly."

"I don't know if those measure the same experiences. *Ma basta*, as you used to say. Come inside the common room. The guests will still be out and about in the city and will not return until this evening."

Just then the porter brought in Alessandra's trunks and set them down inside the office. Alessandra thanked and tipped him, and then turned back to Beatriz. "Unpacking can wait until I've rested a bit."

Alessandra followed as Beatriz walked into the common room. She was pleased to see that Beatriz walked like a woman much younger than 62. *No limping, no shuffling, no huffing and puffing,* she thought. Both women were slim, tall and with hardly a trace of gray hair. Their faces were slightly round and almost wrinkle free. They each had green eyes and an olive complexion. They looked enough alike to be sisters.

The common room was beautifully decorated—a large, rectangular Kurdish carpet covered the middle of the room. The carpet was dark red and purple. Along its six-inch-wide borders were depictions of village life. The walls of the room were whitewashed. Along the walls were low Turkish divans. On each divan were two cushions made of Turkish kilims stuffed with wool. On each of the walls were hung two large kilims. The kilims were predominantly dark orange in color, threaded throughout with brilliant silk yarn.

Alessandra was astonished. "I am so impressed with what you've done with this room! When I left, I told my mother I hoped she would do something about the rather austere common room with a worn carpet."

"Well, our mothers started the project and enlisted my aid. I don't recall for sure but I think your father was still working at his office in town. My father was working at the shipping warehouse at the Port.

"Catarina and Mariana had hired boys to help us keep an eye out for merchant ships unloading their bales of textiles. Your mother found this carpet when we were observing a ship's cargo being unloaded. The caravel had come all the way from Persia. At least several dozen carpets were being taken off the ship and unrolled for airing out. Together our mothers found four others. You should have seen those two intrepid sisters! They engaged the ship's purser in a spirited bout of bargaining before he finally gave in and agreed to their offers. He even agreed to hire a cart for them to be transported all the way to the inn, almost a mile!"

Alessandra knelt down, lifted one corner of the carpet and rubbed her hand across the surface. Then she carefully examined the knotting underneath. "This must be at least 50 years old!"

Beatriz laughed. "It's older than that. We had it examined by two of the carpet merchants in the city, and they agreed it had to be more than 100 years old."

Alessandra stood and stretched. Beatriz said, "Well, my dear Alessandra. Why don't I show you the room your mother first let to your father when he arrived all disheveled from the future."

Alessandra's eyes opened wide and she looked around. Then she smiled. "Don't talk like that. What if someone heard you!"

"Don't worry. Neither your mother nor I have ever told that story to anyone, except for my mother of course. Mariana could hardly keep a secret from her sister!"

Alessandra followed Beatriz upstairs and down the hall to the last room. Alessandra walked to the window and took in the view. "You have expanded the vegetable garden; and look at those eggplants! I only started seeing them in the Padua marketplace a few years ago."

"We started seeing eggplant here about 20 years ago. I remember them being offloaded from a ship from India. We didn't know how to cook them but we learned!"

Alessandra turned away from the window and hugged Beatriz again. Beatriz said, "When you wrote me with the news of your retirement and the upcoming voyage home, I was confused when you said something about your search. Did you mean you would search for a house when you came home? I immediately started looking for a house for you and found several you should take a look at when you're ready. Oh, and I will take you to your parents' resting place in the family crypt. Father Rodrigo, by the way, is still in charge of the church cemetery."

"Yes, I would very much like to see Father Rodrigo and the cemetery. He must be very old now. I think it was about 34 years ago when he arranged for my mom to be buried in the same crypt as my dad."

"Yes, he is pretty old; mid-sixties, I would guess. He keeps talking about retiring and moving back to Oporto, where he was born."

"I hope he gets his wish. But I think you misunderstood me when I wrote that I wanted to start my search. I didn't mean search for a house. I meant that once I began my journey home, I would search for the mosque in Zeila that my father promised would become his book's home.

"Now that that task has been accomplished, I have a surprise for you. What would you say to me becoming your 'inn-mate,' so to speak? After all, you and I are co-owners and partners in this worthy establishment. What do you say to that?"

Beatriz's eyes widened. Then she smiled. "I don't know what to say. Except yes! Yes, I would love it. I love you cousin!" She hugged Alessandra again. She stepped back, rubbed Alessandra's shoulders and said, "You know those two large suites above the reception area?"

"Certainly, I recall them. I lived in one with my parents."

"Well, I've been living in the one my family lived in. You may recall that both rooms have large, back-facing windows looking out on the garden. The one that you and your parents lived in is the way it was when your mother lived there after your dad died. Before your confusing letter, I had hoped you would move back into that room. Let me show you."

"But who will attend to the reception desk?"

"I will have my assistant Diogo keep an eye on it. Let's go!"

"If it wouldn't be too much trouble for Diogo, could you ask him to get a porter to carry my trunks upstairs?"

"Certainly." Beatriz and Alessandra walked back to the reception desk, and Beatriz asked Diogo to get a porter and watch the desk. Then the two cousins walked hand in hand to the office, through the door and up the stairs to the two suites. Beatriz stopped at the top of the stairs and said, "Let me first show you my suite."

Beatriz opened the door and said, "Behold, the `Catarina and Gonçalo Lopes suite!'"

"It's so beautiful! And so much larger than I remember."

"That's because when my father died, my mother sold most of his seafaring memorabilia, which took up much of the space in our lounge."

"And look at this gorgeous carpet! Is it one of the four others that our mothers bought from the ship?"

"Yes, exactly."

"And where are the other three?"

"One is rolled up in our storeroom"

"And the other two?"

"Ah, I was just getting to that. Come with me." Beatriz led Alessandra out of her bedroom, down the hall and into the bedroom that belonged to Mariana, Horacio and Alessandra.

Alessandra was overwhelmed and forgot about the carpets. She felt like she had just traveled back in time to her youth. Her eyes feasted on the large apartment, some 60 feet from the entrance to the far wall with the two huge windows looking out onto the garden. Immediately in front of her she could see the entrances to the bathroom and master bedroom on the left, and the other bedroom, library and lounge on the right.

Beatriz said, "When you left for Padua, your parents left your bedroom unchanged. And when Horacio died, your mom left his desk, books and correspondence intact. Shall we go into their bedroom first?"

Alessandra nodded and followed her cousin. She walked to her father's desk and sat in his chair. She turned to Beatriz and said, "I feel like I've travelled back in time."

Beatriz was leaning against the edge of a large table that was covered with Horacio's map of the Somali coast. "Well, speaking of time travel, your mom and my parents pestered your dad repeatedly to tell stories of his life before he came to live with Mariana, so to speak. And you pestered him, too, of course. After you left and took his book and astrolabe with you, he talked even more about his earlier life."

Alessandra nodded as she continued handling her father's writing materials and the letters he had organized on the desk. Beatriz said, "The one thing he never talked about was his reason for insisting that you take his book and the astrolabe with you when you left for Padua. Did he ever explain that to you?"

Alessandra set down a pile of papers she had been holding and said, "Yes, he did. He was worried about his health and my mom's health. He was 87 and my mom was 75 when I left for university. He wanted to make sure his book and astrolabe wouldn't be lost when he and my mom passed away. They insisted I take them to keep them safe."

Beatriz smiled. "So, you were able to keep them safe, I see. I can't wait to see the astrolabe. He talked so much about the astrolabe and how history took a new path after he broke one of the silver wires when he fell."

Alessandra chuckled and said, "And I'm the beneficiary of that new path. Had he never fallen and broken the wire, he wouldn't have met and married my mom, and I would never have come into existence."

The blood seemed to drain from Beatriz's face. "I never thought of that. And if your dad had managed to return to the future, that would mean your mom would not have asked my parents and me to come and join her in this magnificent *Funduq Mendes*." Beatriz was silent for a few seconds then said, "It seems to me that the task your father has asked you to undertake is fraught with risk."

But Alessandra was no longer listening. She had opened an envelope in her father's desk with her name on it. She was reading what to Beatriz looked like several pages in handwriting she recognized as Horacio's. "What's the matter? You like you're going to faint! You're pale as a sheet. Here, let's get you over to the bed."

But Alessandra shook her head and stayed seated. Tears were in her eyes, and the color still had not returned to her face. "I just can't believe this. How could this be?" She raised up the papers and read them again slowly, aloud:

"My dear Alessandra, my treasure:

"If you are reading this it means you have returned from your teaching career at the University of Padua. Your mother and I are very proud of your accomplishments, and we know you will enjoy your retirement as your cousin Beatriz's partner in running this beautiful inn.

"And now comes the hard part, the part I dreaded telling you all these years. Here it is in a nutshell, an expression from my world. This world you were born in is not my world. Or I should say it is not the world I studied in my career as a history professor.

"You see, when my `Starlight Commune' traveled back in time to 1430 we did not know that not only had we traveled back in time, but we entered a parallel history. Our group returned to 2019 almost immediately to avoid Zheng He's crew in Mogadishu without ever discovering what had happened. Everyone

but me, that is. I was left behind. And soon I noticed things about Mogadishu that were not recorded in the history books I had studied. Not only were they not in the history books, they did not happen! That is to say that the substantial, thriving Catholic community here with its beautiful church, and the substantial, thriving community of Portuguese immigrants never existed in the history of my world.

"You wrote us a long letter describing your three-stage voyage on caravels and coaches to Padua. We marveled at the beauty of your writing. But you described crews on each stage that never could have existed in the past that I studied in my career. Some of your crewmen were Greek, some were Abyssinian, some were Slavic, some were Nordic and some were even Italian! When I was researching the Middle East in my career, I learned that such diverse crews did not exist. Genoese, Venetians and Turks controlled the Mediterranean. Arabs controlled the Red Sea. The Indian Ocean simply didn't have European ships before Vasco da Gama rounded Africa and sailed up and east to India.

"The biggest shock for me, though not for your mother, was that not only did the University admit you, a Portuguese woman from Mogadishu, as a student, but it later hired you as a professor. In the parallel world I lived in before coming here, those early universities did not even admit women as students, let alone hire them as professors; at least not until the 17th century.

"Of course, I knew nothing about the events you must have experienced after my passing. When you were growing up, I described the only near-future I knew—Ahmad Grañ's war with Abyssinia, Vasco da Gama's journey to India. I even told you the date da Gama would anchor just out of sight of the Port of Mogadishu. I do not know whether or not those historical events will come true in your world. Perhaps parallel worlds are not necessarily completely different from one another.

"On the day that your mother and I dropped you off at the Port to begin your voyage to Padua, I had a vision that the book I entrusted you with would not remain in the archive of the Zeila mosque. It would be taken by Ahmad Grañ as a talisman he hoped would ensure his success in his war against Abyssinia. But his hopes would be dashed, he would be killed, and the book would travel into the future from that point on. It would end up in Hawaii to be found in the 21ˢᵗ

century by my former colleague João da Gama and our Starlight Commune. I realized only then that the book must be altered in such a way that the future Starlight Commune will not consider it as anything other than an interesting artifact. I should have realized at the outset that if the Starlight Commune obtained the unedited book, and managed to follow the time-travel directions for repairing the spherical astrolabe, they might travel back in time and create a never-ending loop.

"The note you appended to it must be removed and all references to the astrolabe as a time machine must also be removed. As I write this, I of course do not know whether you will succeed in giving the astrolabe to da Gama. If you do, it will most likely end up in a museum in Portugal. And if you have removed reference to it from my book, then my colleague in the 21st century, João da Gama, will not search for it. Of course, if Vasco da Gama does not donate it to a museum but instead passes it on to another Portuguese mariner, then it will remain forever lost.

"The importance of these tasks I am asking you to undertake is that they will prevent the Starlight Commune from traveling to your world (or a parallel world) and changing it. I do not know what that might precipitate. I shudder at the possible danger that would entail.

"I am very proud of you, my darling daughter. I pray you will continue to experience a happy and productive life in Mogadishu, our Mogadishu.

"Your devoted father, Horacio.

Alessandra set down the letter and looked at Beatriz. Beatriz got up and said, "I'm going downstairs and brew a pot of tea. Would you like some?"

"Yes. I'm feeling a little shaky. I don't know if I can walk just yet. Would you mind bringing the pot upstairs?"

"Certainly." Beatriz left the bedroom.

Alessandra stood, walked to the bed and lay down. The idea that this world, her world, was only one of other parallel worlds frightened her. Then she imagined what her parents must have felt keeping that secret from her and Beatriz; from everyone, probably. *What about Father Rodrigo and his church? What about all the diversity of*

Mogadishu? Will it eventually disappear for the same reason it never came to be in the parallel world? Do similar events take place in parallel worlds because of some sort of probability?

Beatriz came back into her bedroom and set the tea on Horacio's desk. Alessandra said, "You know, I think you and I analyze things the same way. I'm sure you just now thought of things like the church, Father Rodrigo, and our friends. Do you see any reason they should be let in on my father's little secret? I don't." She paused as she poured their tea.

Beatriz nodded, took a sip and set her cup down. "I think you're going to have some work to do soon."

"Yes, but maybe I can let the plan for the astrolabe play out. I certainly will have to retrieve my father's book and do some editing. From the way he described the tasks I must complete, it appears he may have assumed I wouldn't have travelled to Zeila before I read his letter, and would've edited the book before going to Zeila."

CHAPTER TWENTY:

A NEW FRIEND

Lunch was a communal affair. Six guests including Alessandra were sitting at the long table in the dining room. There were seats for six more but Beatriz explained that they were not expected back from their forays into the city until late afternoon. The guests were interesting. Two were Indian merchants on a buying trip. Two were Kenyan men on their way to Djibouti. And one man was a local Portuguese man who owned a fishing company, Afonso Escobar. Alessandra couldn't resist asking the Portuguese man about his business. He looked to be no older than 35. He was slim, wore his hair short and was beardless.

After the lunch guests introduced themselves and busied themselves with their meal, Alessandra asked the Portuguese man, "So, Mr. Escobar, have you been in business in Mogadishu long?"

"Not very long at all. I bought the business four months ago from a man who was retiring."

"And what about before that? Did you come here from Portugal?"

Escobar smiled and said, "In a manner of speaking, yes. Indirectly. I had been an Arabic interpreter on one of Vasco da Gama's ships that left Portugal last year. Our small fleet rounded the Cape of Good Hope and sailed up the East African coast as far as Malindi. The

Captain granted my request to remain on shore at Malindi after I had assisted him in negotiating a trade agreement with the ruler."

Alessandra knew she had to be careful talking about Vasco da Gama, at least not about his voyages. "I'm Portuguese myself and learned a little about that man from my tutors. People seemed to think he was destined for greatness as a mariner. But how did you come to speak Arabic?"

"I had learned Arabic when I lived in the Congo for a few years. When I returned to Portugal and learned da Gama was outfitting a fleet for a voyage to India, I signed on."

Alessandra realized this man might be of some assistance in her plan to meet da Gama. "When did these negotiations take place?"

"It was the middle of last April."

"That wasn't long ago at all! Were you planning on remaining at Malindi?"

Escobar smiled sheepishly and said, "At first I thought I would wait there for the Captain to pick me up on his return voyage home which he estimated would be the following January. But to tell you the truth, the voyage around the Cape was so dangerous, and the crews on each of the ships became so sick, that I decided against returning to Portugal. Instead, I decided I would hire on as crew on an African dhow to take me to Mogadishu. I was in no hurry, but the dhow was a fast one—the trip took less than five days."

"Interesting. I know nothing about dhows. How many men are needed to sail one?"

"I have to say, traveling like that was delightful. The crew consisted of eight men including me. They weren't shocked that I spoke Arabic. Maybe they thought I was an Arab. I don't know if they thought I was Muslim. The subject never came up. Everyone was very busy sleeping when they weren't working hard."

"You say you signed on as a crew member. Did you have experience sailing?

"I had learned to sail in my youth. The other crew members were very happy to let me work alongside them with the sails and steering."

"But why did you decide to go to Mogadishu? Surely you had never heard of it in Portugal."

"That was true of everyone but me. The Captain knew nothing of the African coast before we departed Oporto, nor did the crew on his ships. I had read descriptions of Mogadishu by the Arab explorers Ibn Khaldun and Ibn Battuta, but even those intrepid travelers didn't have much to say about the city. When I told the Captain about those travelers' superficial descriptions, he wasn't convinced the city would be safe for Christians.

"It was the people of Malindi who told me how prosperous and tolerant of foreigners Mogadishu was. As soon as I arrived here, I decided I could live here for the rest of my life."

Alessandra smiled, nodded and said, "I wholeheartedly agree! I'm glad you feel at home here. You say you bought a fishing company. That must have been fortuitous, indeed."

"No, I believe it was as if God smiled on me and gave me a gift I could treasure for the rest of my life."

Alessandra noticed that the other guests had finished their meals and were getting up from the table. Beatriz was watching her from the kitchen with a puzzled look. Alessandra said, "Mr. Escobar, I see we have neglected our food. I apologize for taking so much of your time."

"Not at all. I've enjoyed talking with you. And why are you in Mogadishu?"

"I recently retired from a professorship in Padua and have returned home to Mogadishu. I am co-owner of this inn with my cousin, Beatriz."

Escobar was surprised. "This is your home? It's a long way from Padua. I'm sure there is an interesting story there. Perhaps we can talk more, but I must get back to the docks. Please stop by and we can continue our conversation." He gave Alessandra directions to his office at the docks, and the two of them finished their meals.

Both of them stood and stepped away from the table. Alessandra said, "I would certainly like to continue this discussion. Be careful in these waters; the currents can be dangerous."

As Afonso walked out of the inn, Beatriz hurriedly took off her apron, tossed it to the kitchen assistant, and walked up to Alessandra. "Come with me," she said with a giggle. "We have a lot to talk about."

Alessandra chuckled and squeezed Beatriz's hand. "Yes, we certainly do!"

Settling In

"So, what was that all about? Tell me all about him. This is the first time I've seen him in the restaurant."

Alessandra said, "His story is very fascinating, and it gives me an idea."

"What idea? What are you talking about?"

"Let's unpack and I'll explain when you see what's in my smaller trunk."

"Ooh, I love mysteries!"

Diogo had delivered Alessandra's trunks in the meantime. The two women carried them into Alessandra's bedroom and opened the smaller one. Beatrix eyed a large, round object completely wrapped in a blanket. "I'll bet that's the spherical astrolabe."

"Good guess, genius."

Beatriz laughed. "Another of your dad's favorite expressions!" Turning serious she said, "You said you sent Horacio's book off on the `first stage of its journey to the future,' is what I recall you saying. That's bound to be a great story. Tell me about it."

Before answering, Alessandra took the wrapped astrolabe and set it on the desk. She removed the blanket, said the astrolabe upright, and said, "Voilà!"

Beatriz walked around to look at it from both sides of the desk. "That's a beautiful machine! Look at all those fine silver bands and silver wires. The wires pass through the little gold globe. Your dad said one of the silver wires is broken inside the globe. But I can't see how you could tell."

"That's because the little globe originally had been opened to allow the modifications inside. Then the wires were threaded through in a certain pattern, and the globe soldered shut. To repair the broken one, a highly trained artisan would have to use modern tools to open the globe, then solder the wire back together and re-solder the globe. My dad couldn't find anyone who had the tools or solder because those things didn't exist yet."

Turning away from the astrolabe, Beatriz said, "Now you have two stories to tell me: what did you do with the book, and what will you do with the astrolabe."

"First things first. I don't know if my dad ever said anything about the book or how it would end up in the future. Here's the short version. My dad had a vision that a large mosque in the Somali coastal city of Zeila would be a great home for his book."

"Why Zeila? It's one of Somalia's ports, very near Djibouti."

"As he wrote in his letter, my dad realized its connection to what he knew as a retired history professor. He had read about a great Somali warrior named Ahmad Grañ who would arise in the 16th century and challenge Abyssinia's hegemony in the Horn. My dad's vision was that Grañ would visit Zeila. Not only visit. The mosque's Imam would offer Grañ the book."

"Yes, he said that in the letter. But why would a warrior be interested in a book?"

"The histories of the Horn of Africa all described Grañ as a very superstitious man. My dad interpreted his vision to mean Grañ might believe the book to be a talisman guaranteeing the success of his campaign."

"A talisman? Did Grañ have a talisman in your dad's 'parallel' history?"

"History doesn't say. My dad and other historians suspected he did. Some sources say he was superstitious. No surprise there; many people were, especially warriors and rulers. But finally, according to the historical record, Grañ was killed by a Portuguese rifleman in the service of Abyssinian Emperor Galawdewos in Grañ's final battle in 1543."

"If the talisman was the book, what happened to it after that?"

"My father wasn't sure. What the record did show was that Grañ's widow would flee the battle with hundreds of soldiers and her husband's possessions. My dad thought she would take the book with her. She would remarry in the city of Harar. He thought she might find and take the book with her there as well."

As Alessandra paused to take a breath, Beatriz was sitting up straight drumming her fingers on the arms of the chair. She asked, "How certain are you that any of those events that happened in your father's world, the world he lived in before he came here, will take place?"

"I'm not sure at all, of course. But I think I should do what he suggested in the letter."

Beatriz asked, "So you went to Zeila? Are you going back?"

"Yes. It was a short and easy task. My ship had docked for two days for unloading and loading, so I went into the town and found the *Masjid al-Qiblatayn*. The head Imam agreed to keep my father's book safely stored in the archive. I could see that the Imam was struck by my father's hope that his book would be placed in the archive. So, I think I should be able to return and tell the Imam that I need to correct some things in the book. I can't see why he would object."

Beatriz stood and walked over again to the astrolabe. "Now, you said earlier your father believed this astrolabe would embark on a world-wide journey with the assistance of Vasco da Gama. And that journey would begin next January 2, is that right?"

Alessandra bit her lip. She took a deep breath and said, "This is the tricky part. My dad knew, from having read da Gama's ship's log, that the fleet would drop anchor off the Port of Mogadishu on the evening of January 2, 1499, and continue on its journey home the next morning. But nobody in this city knows that. How could anyone know that da Gama's fleet would return from India at that precise time? No one but me. But now I'm not even sure of that in this parallel world to my father's.

"Also, I don't know if I would be able to hire a boat to take me out to da Gama's fleet. I mean, any sane boat owner would think it suicidal to do that. And the biggest problem is this: how would I present the spherical astrolabe to da Gama, if none of his ships would venture into the harbor?"

Beatriz turned back to Alessandra. "Well, I think I know what you've got in mind. It has something to do with the young gentleman you were having lunch with, am I right?"

"Yes, you're right. The gentleman's name is Afonso Escobar. He was an interpreter on one of da Gama's ships. Da Gama granted his request to remain in Malindi. Escobar didn't want to go any further with da Gama's fleet. Da Gama wanted to reward him for his interpretive assistance in the trade agreement with the leaders of the city. But rather than remain in Malindi, Mr. Escobar instead decided to travel north to Mogadishu and stay. He bought a fishing operation here and is very happy. I don't believe he has any intention of getting back on board one of da Gama's ships, even if the fleet made a port call at Mogadishu, which it won't."

Alessandra stood and stretched. She turned to Beatriz and hugged her. "I think I should unpack and take a nap. Tomorrow will be a busy day."

The Big City

After breakfast the next morning, Beatriz made sure the inn staff understood the day's agenda and escorted Alessandra out onto the streets of Mogadishu. "I'll show you where the church is."

Alessandra stopped walking and said, "You seem to have forgotten that I lived here for the first 20 years of my life and my mother and I attended services in that church many times. My father was not as religious but he occasionally came with us."

"Well, cousin, you will be shocked at how much the city has grown and changed. And the city's *Santo Condestável* church is healthier than ever. That's where we're going, to visit our parents' crypt."

"You mean your parents and my parents are buried in the same mausoleum?"

"Yes. It's a beautiful small building. Like a little Roman temple."

Alessandra noticed that Beatriz seemed anxious. "Do I detect a bit of concern on your part? Does something worry you?"

Beatriz paused. "Well, after hearing what your father wrote in the letter, I wonder whether Christian institutions here are going to be under siege in the future."

"The future is not promising, at least the future my father came from. As I said, whether the future he came from remains the same as our future is an open question. Which brings me to the subject of our family mausoleum. We need to decide, you and I together, what should happen to our mausoleum. My father made sure I understood what the near future might portend for Mogadishu. If Ahmad Grañ arises and is subsequently defeated by the Abyssinians 45 years from now, Christians in Mogadishu will be put in a difficult position. It is safe to say Catholics, especially Portuguese Catholics, will be driven from this country and from Abyssinia in the mid-1600's. And the few remaining Christian communities outside of Abyssinia will be under siege by Muslims for several hundred years thereafter.

"But we need to keep in mind that those events might not happen. Remember what my father said in his letter. The world we live in, with its harmony among different religions and ethnic groups, its strong Catholic community here in Mogadishu, might be so resilient that the type of fanaticism represented by militant Islam and Ahmad Grañ will not arise. In any event we need to prepare for the worst."

Beatriz stared at Alessandra. "I was afraid of something like that happening. Will Christian buildings and shrines here be destroyed?"

"In the face of militant Islam, most likely. But here's an idea. Tell me what you think. Why don't we ask the priest, Father Rodrigo, to arrange for our parents' remains to be moved and the mausoleum removed? That shouldn't be a problem, don't you think?"

"A problem? Of course, that might be a problem! I can't imagine where we could put the mausoleum. But I guess that makes more sense than waiting for the type of future that unrolled in your father's world."

When the women arrived at the church, Alessandra said, "It's even more beautiful than it was when I used to attend. The grounds seem to be more extensive and with many more plantings. The trees are fully mature now." Then she added, "I don't think we should tell Father Rodrigo what my father said in the letter to me."

Beatriz nodded and led Alessandra to the church entrance and said, "The Sext prayer service won't begin until noon. I would guess Father Rodrigo is in his office preparing for it."

They entered, dipped their fingers in the holy water font, crossed themselves and walked through the church. The priest's office was behind the altar, and the door was on the right. When they entered, Father Rodrigo looked up from his desk and smiled. He stood and faced the women. "Ah, Miss Lopes, so nice to see you. And please introduce me to your friend."

"This is my cousin Alessandra Fuente. She is the daughter of the late Mariana Mendes and Horacio Fuente."

The priest smiled. "Oh, I am so pleased to meet you Miss Fuente. I knew your parents. Fond memories. And I found your father's stories quite fascinating!" He winked, turned back to Beatriz and said, "Please, won't both of you have a seat? I have a little time before I convene the Sext service." After the women sat down, he said, "Would you like some tea? I just took a pot off the coals."

Beatriz and Alessandra nodded and smiled. Father Rodrigo got up and walked into the little office kitchen. Alessandra turned to Beatriz and said, "What do you suppose that wink was supposed to mean?"

"What wink? I didn't see a wink. Are you sure it was a wink?"

"Yes, it was a wink, a knowing wink. What does he know? I thought you said you and your parents never talked about the future to anyone else."

"Well, you know, he's the family priest, after all."

"Are you saying you told the priest in the confessional?"

"No, of course not. Our families enjoyed listening to your father tell his stories to Father Rodrigo. They became good friends. I think you needn't worry about him telling anyone else. Sacred Vows and all that."

Father Rodrigo came back in carrying an ornate tray made of some type of dark brown wood inlaid with ivory figures of elephants. On it were three Arab tea glasses, lumps of rock sugar, and a small teapot filled with concentrated black tea sitting atop a larger pot of just-boiled water. He set the tray down on the little side table between the women's chairs and said, "This is black tea that local importers have obtained from Persia. I have fallen in love with it."

Alessandra and Beatriz filled their glasses with half concentrated tea and half boiling water. Father Rodrigo asked, "Would you like to view your parents' crypt after we're finished here?"

Alessandra said, "Yes, certainly, I would love to. But first tell me, what kind of stories did my father talk about?"

Father Rodrigo sat back in his desk chair and folded his hands on his lap. "They were quite stunning stories, but for anyone who didn't know Horacio the stories would be simply too strange to believe."

"But you believed him? Did he tell you he was writing a memoir?"

"Oh, yes. But he never showed it to me; or to anyone, as far as I know, before he sent you off with it to Padua."

"Did he describe how he ended up here? Stranded here?"

"Yes, he did. Something about a broken mariner's device he called a spherical astrolabe. I'd heard of the common astrolabe but never a spherical astrolabe. Again, that was something he never showed us before handing it over to you. I assumed that because your father and his time-traveling colleagues were history professors whose fields were East Africa and the Middle East, it was logical they would choose Mogadishu as their destination. It's a multiethnic hub of commerce with Europe, India, China, Arabia, Persia and all of Africa."

Alessandra realized she had been holding her breath. She normalized her breathing and took another sip of her tea. "You must have wondered why on Earth my father wanted me take those things with me to university."

"I did. And he told me; or at least part of the reason. He was worried about his health, your mother's health, and what might happen to the book and astrolabe if they remained here when your parents passed. But I never understood what he intended you to do with them."

Beatriz looked over at Alessandra to see how she was taking these revelations. Then she turned and said, "Father Rodrigo, Alessandra and I want to talk to you about our family crypt."

Alessandra said, "Yes, but first let me tell you that I have given my father's book to the imam of a mosque in Zeila to be placed it the archives. But I need to return to the mosque to make some corrections to the book. I also have the task of handing the astrolabe over to Vasco da Gama."

"I don't understand. Vasco da Gama? Here? What do you mean?"

"Yes, here. My father told me da Gama will be dropping anchor outside the Bay of Mogadishu next January second. I must meet him and give him the astrolabe. I hope he will receive it and will use it in its usual function, that is to say, as an advanced mariner's navigation device, not a time machine. It no longer works as a time machine, anyway, and cannot be restored as one with local tools and science."

The priest sat back and drank the last of his tea. He poured himself another blend of tea mixed with hat water before looking at Alessandra expectantly. "I do hope you're going to tell me how you plan on meeting him. I hadn't heard of him since he was currying favor with the King of Portugal."

Alessandra set her own cup down and said, "First let's go to our parents' crypt and talk about the future in a different light."

The priest stood and gestured to the side door of his office that led to the church cemetery.

Once they were standing in front of the crypt and had said their silent prayers, Alessandra said, "Father Rodrigo, our parents' crypt cannot remain."

The priest and Beatriz looked startled. Rodrigo asked, "Whatever do you mean, it cannot remain?"

"I mean that the crypt, the coffins, the beautiful marble structure, none of it should remain."

"I'm afraid I don't understand why. Please go on."

"Father, you've already heard Horacio's stories of how he came to be stranded here. Did he ever talk of the future? I mean the future 25 years from now, not the future 500 years from now."

"No, not in any detail. He said he would let his daughter fill me in. So, what does the near future hold for your crypt and mausoleum, or indeed for this church and this city?"

"Well, Father, I don't know how much Professor Horacio Fuente told you, and I know you'll find it hard to imagine, but the history books in his time said that in the middle of the next century—that is to say 25 years from now in the 16th century—the social and political order in the Horn of Africa will begin to crumble. And in the century after that, there will be no safe place for Catholic Christianity anywhere in East Africa. Wars for political gain, for religious hegemony, will sweep away all our beloved institutions. Not even the Orthodox Christian Abyssinians will allow Catholics to reenter their kingdom."

The priest looked shaken. He said, "I know I should believe you, but I cannot quite bring myself to accept that all this will be swept away."

Beatriz looked at Alessandra, then back at the priest. She said, "Let's go back inside and my cousin will explain what she thinks should be done."

The cousins walked on either side of the priest, since he looked somewhat unstable on his feet. Once seated back in the church office, Alessandra said, "What I propose is this. This noble church should remove the grand columns and the family mausoleum from the churchyard, leaving just the four coffins. I hate to be morbid, but the remains inside those coffins can by now be placed in four individual marble ossuaries.

"The next thing that must be done, the hardest thing, will be for me to find a way to approach Vasco da Gama's ships and ask that he take the four ossuaries as 'passengers,' so to speak, and transport them back to Portugal, which is his destination."

Again, the priest was stunned. The blood had run out of his face. For that matter, Beatriz was similarly affected. "Alessandra, you didn't tell me all this before."

"Well, I hadn't thought it all the way through. But now I realize that my father's astrolabe will have companions on his way to Portugal—his remains, my mother's remains, and the remains of your parents, that is if you agree."

Beatriz spoke when she saw that the priest was not yet in any condition to comment on what her cousin had just said. "Alessandra, what you have just said makes no sense. Won't it be hard enough even to approach da Gama's fleet, let alone talk to the Captain himself and convince him to transport four marble ossuaries all the way to Portugal?"

At this point, Father Rodrigo's complexion had recovered most of its coloring and he found words. "If he will be amenable to transporting the ossuaries, do you think he would be amenable to taking me with him, perhaps as their `guardian,' so to speak?"

The question stunned the cousins. Beatriz found her voice first, but barely more than a whisper: "Father, you can't be serious. Leave your beloved church without its pastor?"

"I was planning on retiring anyway. Soon. Not only that, but I've been longing to return to my beloved ancestral home in Oporto. Maybe this scheme that your cousin is proposing will be the means of accomplishing that. The church will not be without a priest; several work here already as deacons."

Alessandra once again found her voice. "Father, I think you have just made a brilliant suggestion. The Captain would definitely decide his ship needs a priest. And he would certainly welcome the gift of the spherical astrolabe. The trip down the east coast of Africa, around the Cape, up the west coast of Africa, and to Oporto would be extremely dangerous without it.

"I haven't had a chance here to bring up a most amazing fact— Vasco da Gama's former Arabic interpreter is now living in Mogadishu. He is the owner of some fishing boats. I met him at lunch yesterday at Beatriz's inn. I wouldn't be surprised if you had met him also. His name is Afonso Escobar."

"Ah, yes, Mr. Escobar. He has been attending church services lately, not regularly, but often enough that we have had several conversations. Only about the Port, the city and the fishing conditions."

Alessandra said, "Well, Mr. Escobar invited me to call on him at the Port. Perhaps I'll ask him if he would be willing to ferry us out to da Gama's fleet."

CHAPTER TWENTY-ONE

MEETING AT THE SAÕ GABRIEL

Alessandra did not rush in getting to know Afonso Escobar. After all, she had five months before Vasco da Gama's fleet would drop anchor off the Port of Mogadishu. But she made a point of allowing him to show off his little fleet of fishing boats. He introduced Alessandra to all his fishing crew. He even took her out on the boat he was most proud of. It was almost 30 feet long and had two oarlocks on each side. At the rear he had installed a small cabin covered with sturdy, waterproofed canvas. "I don't often use it as a fishing boat. More of a pleasure boat to take my friends on tours outside the harbor." His other four boats were 20 feet long. Six men manned three of them and 10 men, including Afonso, manned the fourth one.

When she wasn't paying visits to Afonso, she focused on getting Father Rodrigo ready for the voyage home, just in case Vasco da Gama would agree to take him on as a passenger, or perhaps as the chaplain, she thought.

The priest was visibly excited at the prospect of going home, even though he would have to see that the ossuaries were delivered to their permanent home. Alessandra had asked him if he was familiar with the *Igreja de Santa Clara* in Oporto. His answer was an enthusiastic yes. He had prayed in it many times in his youth.

Alessandra told him her mother's parents had been members of that church before coming to Mogadishu.

Father Rodrigo was also excited at the possibility of sailing home on a large ship. He was an accomplished sailor, and in his youth had worked on his uncle's sailboat on the Douro River and in the Atlantic off of Oporto. As he began training the two deacons in the tasks necessary to maintaining the church, the grounds, and the community, he imagined the proposal he would make to Vasco da Gama—to take him aboard as ship's priest. Or a deck hand! The oldest deck hand in the world!

Alessandra was enjoying her new life as an innkeeper alongside her beloved cousin Beatriz. At the end of their busy days, they had many late-night conversations when the inn was quiet and the restaurant and bar were in the able hands of the long-time staff. Alessandra loved hearing Beatriz's stories of how she had been groomed by Mariana and Catarina to take over the operation of the inn. Beatriz had overseen the expansion of the restaurant and kitchen, the improvements to the guest rooms, and the replacement of the carpets and furniture in the common room, library, dining room and office. Running a complex enterprise like the *Funduq Mendes* kept Beatriz full of joy at being alive and compassion for her beloved city, Mogadishu. Alessandra knew Beatriz well enough that she didn't need to ask lots of questions about her personal life. Besides, Beatriz often raised that subject herself.

On a chilly night in late September the two women lay on the carpet in front of the fireplace in Alessandra's library. Beatriz mused, "I used to ask myself why I hadn't found a man, that special man who would love me and care for me. But the more I got to know men as customers, guests, businessmen, and government officials, I decided I didn't really want to tie my life to a man's life. I have enough work to do here, work that I love, by the way. I don't need to make my life more complicated, and in all likelihood more stressful."

"I certainly understand, dear Beatriz. Maybe some men feel

threatened, or at least uncomfortable, when confronted by a strong, independent woman who owns and operates a business. I also decided to remain a single, independent woman. Men sometimes don't know what to make of a woman who occupies a position equal to theirs. I'm not talking about male assumptions of the proper marital relationship. My experience with men was almost entirely based on the men I worked with, taught, and hired to transport me places, such as my voyages to Padua and back. I think I must have projected an air of independence that discouraged men. And I also think I just never was that interested in men. That sounds terrible, I know."

"Well, it doesn't sound terrible at all, and I think you know it. You don't need to pretend otherwise." She and Alessandra burst out laughing. Then for the next few minutes they gazed into the fire and listened to the hissing and popping of the firewood as it was consumed. Beatriz got up, stretched, and said, "I think I'm going to go to bed. Do you want me to ask Andres to come up and bank the fire so you can leave it?"

"No, I think I'll stay here for a little while longer. Maybe I'll write some more in my journal. Maybe I'll work on my strategy for broaching a difficult subject with my fisherman friend, the good Afonso Escobar." She stood and gave Beatriz a kiss. "Sleep well, my dear."

It turned out that Alessandra didn't have a strategy in mind. As the weeks went by, she tried to spend more time with Afonso in the hope that an idea would come to mind. She surprised him, and herself, one day by speaking to him in Arabic. He laughed and replied in Arabic, "Ah, I had forgotten what you told me about the subjects you taught. And it makes sense you would have learned Arabic here in Mogadishu. Didn't you also tell me you taught English? How did you learn English in a city with no English speakers?"

"Yes, I taught English. And no, there were no English speakers here. Except for my father. He had learned it growing up and insisted I learn it here. He taught it to me himself."

"And astronomy? Did he teach you that as well?"

"Not really. But he supplemented my tutor's lessons with his own knowledge of how mariners traveled the oceans by using devices such as the spherical astrolabe."

"Ah, yes, the queen of astrolabes. I remember how worried my Captain was when he was unable to obtain one for our voyage. You say your father had one?"

"Yes, and gave me many astronomy lessons supplemented by that device."

"I don't understand why he would have such a device. You say he was a history professor. How would a history professor obtain a spherical astrolabe?"

Alessandra realized she had spoken too freely and quickly invented something. "Many years ago, a client of his gave him one as payment for some work he did. My father kept it on his desk." She hoped that satisfied Afonso. At any rate he didn't pursue the subject.

Finally, Alessandra came up with an idea of how to meet da Gama and present him with the astrolabe. It was the result of a conversation she and Afonso were having in early December. Afonso had taken Alessandra on a fishing trip in his large boat just beyond the mouth of the Bay. As Afonso's men were rowing the boats up to the pier, he turned to Alessandra and asked, "Alessandra, something else puzzles me about you. You had a long career as an academic in Italy, yet now you seem to take an unusual interest in my fishing activities. Could you tell me what has generated that interest?"

Alessandra decided to tell him the truth, or at least part of the truth. "Afonso, I am very fond of keeping company with you now that I have returned to my home. Besides my cousin Beatriz, you are my only friend here. After spending many years in Italy, I have come home to a place I hardly know, and the friends I had in my youth have either died or moved elsewhere. But you are right to be puzzled by my interest in your fishing activities. My father gave me a task to undertake when I left to pursue my education in Padua."

Afonso was momentarily distracted by another boat's docking operation. Then he asked, "So, if I'm not being too nosy, what is the task you have been given?"

"I must deliver a valuable object to Vasco da Gama, your former Captain."

Afonso stopped what he was doing. "Vasco da Gama is either in India, or at the bottom of the sea, or on his way back to Malindi, where he dropped me off many months ago. Nobody knows when he will pass this way again. I cannot see how you would be able to meet the Captain."

Alessandra took a deep breath and said, "The great Captain is indeed on his way here, with his fleet intact, and will drop anchor just at the mouth of the bay on the evening of January 2, less than a month from now."

"And how do you know that? Did you have a vision, a dream, what?"

"Neither, although a vision is what I will tell Captain da Gama when we meet. He will not enter the Port out of fear of the unknown. He thinks the city is hostile to Christians. He will spend the night anchored outside the bay and be on his way to Malindi in the morning."

"But you cannot know this! And are you hoping I will take you out to meet him?"

"No. I am hoping you will order four of your crew to row this boat out to where the Captain will be anchored. But I do not think it would be wise for you to be aboard. The Captain might decide to take you prisoner, or at least bring you back on his ship to continue on his journey."

"You still haven't explained why you think you know the precise time of his arrival."

"Dear Afonso, I owe you a full explanation, and you will get one.

But if you will allow me to borrow this worthy craft, with four oarsmen, on that night, I will deliver the thing my father entrusted me with, and will return to the harbor. Then I will tell you the whole story. And the four oarsmen will tell you what they have witnessed."

Afonso sighed, then smiled and said, "And after you tell me the whole story, I will write it down in my journal for all the world to read after I am gone." He helped Alessandra out of the boat and onto the dock. He held her hand and the two of them walked slowly back to the inn.

Show Time

As promised, on the night of January 2, 1499, Afonso had his crew colorfully decorate the large, partially covered fishing boat and place lanterns all around. He was surprised to see Father Rodrigo come walking onto the dock with Alessandra. Not only that, but the priest was carrying baggage as if he were about to embark on a voyage. Alessandra was carrying something large covered by a sheet. Accompanying them were two of the priest's servants each carrying two ossuaries. Afonso said to him, "Father, it looks like you're going on a voyage. Don't tell me you're going to join Vasco da Gama's voyage home." Afonso still couldn't believe that Alessandra's prediction would happen.

"Yes, that's exactly what I hope to do. I've retired from the church and will live out the rest of my days in Oporto, where I was born."

Father Rodrigo was carrying a large cross. The crew secured the cross upright in the bow of the boat backlit by lanterns. The crewmen took the priest's bags and the ossuaries and placed them inside the cabin. Alessandra sat next to them holding the covered astrolabe on her lap. Father Rodrigo stood at the bow next to the backlit cross. It was just after 11 p.m. and a bright, full moon floated above them in a cloudless sky. The crewmen began rowing the boat out of the harbor. About an hour after they passed the last pier, they were astonished to see da Gama's ship, the *Saõ Gabriel*, and the other ships at anchor.

When their boat approached the *Saõ Gabriel* Father Rodrigo loudly hailed the ship in Portuguese. When an astonished sailor appeared at the side of the *Saõ Gabriel*, Father Rodrigo announced himself. "I am Father Rodrigo, pastor of the *Santo Condestável* Catholic church in Mogadishu. I and one of my parishioners wish to have an audience with Captain Vasco da Gama."

The sailor stepped back, walked to the Captain's cabin and informed the Captain.

Curious and suffering from insomnia, da Gama stepped outside his cabin and walked to the side of the ship. He was astonished at the sight of the brightly lit fishing boat. He immediately ordered a rowboat uncovered. The Captain was about to board it when his Arabic interpreter João Peres approached. "Captain, if you don't mind, I would like to accompany you. I will be armed in the event there is treachery." The Captain agreed and they boarded the fishing boat.

Two of the Captain's crewmen rowed the boat next to the garishly decorated fishing boat. Alessandra had come outside holding the astrolabe. Standing on the other side of the cross from Father Rodrigo she said, "Captain da Gama, we are honored that your ships have anchored here. I am Alessandra Fuente, a native of this city. My priest at Mogadishu's *Santo Condestável* church, Father Martim Rodrigo, is here with me.

"The reason for our visit with you is this," holding up the astrolabe she continued, "I have inherited this very valuable maritime navigational instrument, a spherical astrolabe. I offer it to you in the hope that it will enable you to return home to Portugal safely." Alessandra reached across the gap between the two boats and handed the astrolabe to the Captain.

Da Gama held it up and examined it from several angles. After almost a minute he said, "I am astounded at the magnificence of this machine. I am aware of these, but our fleet left Portugal before one could be obtained. We were forced to use charts and an ancient, simpler, astrolabe." Looking up from the astrolabe he asked, "But why are you giving me this valuable instrument?"

"I am giving it to you on behalf of my deceased father, Horacio Aleixandre Fuente. He was a respected historian here in Mogadishu who specialized in the Portuguese explorations on behalf of the Crown. A visiting merchant from Malindi told us of your visit there last April, and that your fleet intended Calcutta as your destination. I hope my father's spherical astrolabe will ensure your safety on the trip home and on many trips thereafter."

Da Gama handed the spherical astrolabe to Mr. Peres and said, "I thank you very much, Milady!" He began to turn away when Peres said something to the Captain in a low voice. The Captain turned back to Alessandra and said, "Mr. João Peres, one of my ship's officers, would like to ask you a few questions."

Mr. Peres asked Alessandra in Arabic, "Miss Fuente, have you lived in Mogadishu all your life?"

Alessandra was stunned to hear Arabic come out of this Portuguese man's mouth. She answered in Arabic, "You surprise me, sir. I did not expect to hear a Portuguese sailor speak the language of Mogadishu and the Middle East. But the answer to your question is I have not lived here all my life. I was born and raised here, but attended the University of Padua for five years. After I graduated, I accepted the offer to teach at the University. I taught for 36 years and recently retired."

Now it was Peres's turn to be surprised. Switching to Portuguese he said, "Padua! How did you manage to do that? What subjects did you teach?"

"I taught Arabic, English and Astronomy."

"First, you surprised me with your fluency in Arabic, which I admit I thought would prove you to be an Arab, rather than

Portuguese. Now you surprise me by speaking perfect Portuguese, and saying you taught English. How did you learn English? Surely, there are no English speakers in Mogadishu."

"You are correct. After my father died, I am the only English speaker left. But from a young age my father had insisted that I study English with a tutor."

The Captain said something to Peres in a low voice. Peres turned back to Alessandra. "Now, I have to say that there is another thing that surprises us, the most surprising thing. How did you know that our fleet would anchor here at this precise time?"

Alessandra conjured up her best blush and sheepish demeanor and said, "All I can say is that two nights ago I had a dream that a Portuguese fleet commanded by the famous Vasco da Gama was returning to Portugal after completing a voyage to India. In my dream, I saw the fleet anchoring off the Port on this very night. My dream was so vivid that it woke me up. I never for a moment doubted the truth of the dream. The next morning, I walked to my church and sought out Father Rodrigo for guidance. He assured me my dream was true because he had a similar dream! Yesterday we arranged this transportation and rowed out here just now."

Mr. Peres was at a loss for words. He thanked Alessandra and turned back to the Captain. As the two of them began to turn away Alessandra said, "Captain da Gama, my parish priest, Father Martim Rodrigo, would like to address you."

Da Gama turned back to the priest and said, "Father Rodrigo, may God grant you long life. I was not aware there was a Catholic community in Mogadishu. But I am happy to hear such good news. Now what is it you would like to say?"

"My Lord, it is my greatest honor to meet you. I, like many of our Portuguese countrymen, have followed your career. And now you are returning from your historic voyage to India! Congratulations on your achievement! If I may be so bold, sir. I would like to ask something of you. My home is Oporto. I would like to return home before I die. If your magnificent ship, the *Saõ Gabriel*, does not have a priest on board, I would ask that you accept me into your service as ship's chaplain. I would also like to take with me four historic ossuaries and deliver them to the *Igreja de Santa Clara* in Oporto."

Vasco da Gama was at a loss for words. But then he smiled. "Surely, this request is inspired by God! My crew and I have been long at sea without the benefit of having a priest on board. You would be most welcome, and the ossuaries as well. You may bring your boat alongside the *Saõ Gabriel* and my crewmen will take you and your precious cargo aboard. We will salute you and your city in the morning! We raise anchor at first light."

Alessandra said, "Most generous Captain, I thank you and thank God for your decision." After Father Rodrigo and the ossuaries were safely transferred, Alessandra's boat turned around. The crew rowed it back to the harbor. Alessandra stood next to the cross and watched the city of her birth come closer.

Let's Begin Again

Alessandra was happy to see Afonso waiting on the dock when she and the crew pulled up an hour after midnight. She knew he had been waiting for two hours. A crewman helped Alessandra off the boat. She expected Afonso to ask what happened to the priest. Instead he smiled and offered his arm as they started walking back to the inn. She did not want to bring up a subject that would be difficult to explain. Instead, she said, "If you still have an appetite, I'll prepare you something to eat at the inn."

"I know you're expecting me to begin asking questions, but I'll wait for you to talk about it when you're ready." Taking a deep breath of the salt air, he said, "I would love something to eat. I was too nervous to eat all day."

Alessandra was relieved at the temporary respite. "Your four crewmen will confirm that they took Father Rodrigo and me to da

Gama's boat about a mile from the port." She smiled and continued. "Captain da Gama accepted his offer to be the ship's chaplain. The Captain said he would salute us when the fleet pulls up anchor at first light in the morning. That's a few hours from now. Let's have an early breakfast and then walk out to the end of the pier."

"But what do you mean he'll salute us? And how will we know when first light is?"

"I think we'll hear the cannon from just about anywhere in the city. But if you like we can stand out on the end of the pier. When we hear the muezzin's call to prayer at dawn, I think the cannon will answer." They both chuckled and slowly made their way to the inn.

Beatriz was waiting for them at the reception counter when they walked in. "Well, I want to hear all about it. If you're hungry, there's some very good chicken stew left over from the dinner meal."

Beatriz heated up the stew as Alessandra and Afonso got comfortable in the lounge.

"I think we have about three hours before first light," Alessandra said.

Beatriz walked in with a tray holding the pot of stew, a loaf of dark bread, butter, bowls and silverware. "What's going to happen at first light?"

"Our skeptical gentleman here doesn't want to believe me that Father Rodrigo and I met Vasco da Gama at his ship just now."

"So, your plan worked, I take it. The Reverend Father is on his way to Portugal?"

"Yes, and he's taking with him the four ossuaries containing the remains of our parents."

Afonso looked from Alessandra to Beatriz and back again. "So, Beatriz, I guess you were in on this plan. Or story. Perhaps you would be willing to explain how Alessandra knew that Vasco da Gama's fleet would anchor beyond the harbor."

Alessandra said, "I'll let my cousin begin the story while I start eating. And I advise you not to let your food get cold."

She and Afonso started eating and listened to Beatriz's story. "Afonso, has my cousin told you much about her parents?"

Setting down his spoon he said, "Only that they immigrated here from Portugal before she was born."

Beatriz chuckled. "Well, there's half a lie right there. Her father most certainly did not immigrate here from Portugal, although he was Portuguese." Alessandra groaned and covered her ears.

Afonso asked, "Do you mean he was born here in Mogadishu?"

"No, I mean he was born in the Hawaiian Islands in the Year of Our Lord, 1954."

Afonso continued eating and in between bites he said, "Go on. This sounds like a very humorous tale. Born in the future on a mysterious island and moved to the past?"

Alessandra finished chewing her bread and smiled. "I can see that my story needs to be filled out before it will become credible."

Beatriz said, "No. I have an idea. You two finish eating and when you're done, let's go upstairs to Alessandra's suite. I think I can show you some things that might convince you."

Alessandra nodded her agreement. After she and Afonso finished, she escorted Afonso and Beatriz upstairs to her rooms. Afonso had never been upstairs and was surprised at the size of the two suites. Alessandra led them into her suite. "Okay, Beatriz, tell us what you want to show Afonso."

"By your leave, cousin dear, would you mind showing him the clothes your father was wearing when he arrived here from the future?"

Alessandra burst out laughing and said, "Of course. Why not?" She opened the door to the huge, walk-in closet and said, "Follow me, please." She walked through her closet and into the storage room that connected her suite and Beatriz's suite. She pulled open a drawer, rummaged through it briefly, and pulled out three items of clothing.

The first was a white tee shirt with a label inside the collar that read "Jockey" on one side and "Made in USA" on the other. The second item was a pair of sandals made out of leather bonded to rubber. The word "Skechers" was embossed on the outside of the back strap, and the words "Made in Viet Nam" were embossed under the top strap. The third item was a pair of black sweatpants with the word "Japan" on one side of a printed cotton label sewn on the inside of the waist band. On the underside of the label were the words "Cotton-Poly Blend" and "Size 34."

Alessandra brought the items over to her bed and spread them out for Afonso to examine. Beatriz smiled and looked at Afonso as he handled each item. He spent a few minutes doing that, then set down the clothing and turned to Alessandra. "I don't suppose you would explain where these items of clothing came from. Or perhaps I should `when' they came from."

Alessandra smiled, "Yes, I'll explain when and where they came from. In the 21st century when these items were manufactured, there is a country called Japan. It consists of a group of islands in the Pacific east of China. Japan is a strong country in the future, with highly developed industries. They manufacture many things, including clothing. The letters USA stand for United States of America, a powerful country west across the Atlantic from Europe. The phrase `cotton-poly blend' describes a blend of two fabrics, cotton and a synthetic fabric called polyester. The phrase `size 34' is a measurement around the waist. The words `Viet Nam' refer to an Asian country near India and China. In the 21st century that country had developed its economy rapidly after recovering from a disastrous war with the United States of America. Skechers is a brand of shoe, including sandals."

After absorbing this barrage of information for several minutes as he picked up and examined each item, Afonso sat down. "So, you say your father was wearing these items when he traveled back in time?"

"Yes, but he wore a Somali *ma'awiis* robe over them to blend in. He had not intended to remain here. He intended to return to the

21st century with the small group of his professor colleagues. But his spherical astrolabe broke when he fell in an alley near the public market. So, he remained here and started a new life."

"And what kind of new life did he start?"

"He was able to find work translating documents and helping clients prepare documents because he spoke Portuguese, Arabic and English."

"And he married your mother?"

"Yes. At first, he rented a room at her inn, this inn. She helped him purchase suitable clothing and shoes and steered clients to him. They married a few years later."

Again, Afonso was at a loss for words. Then he looked up and asked, "What was that you said… that his time machine was a spherical astrolabe? How did he convert a mariner's device into a time machine?"

"He didn't. Or at least he wasn't the first in his group to do so. It seems a colleague in his group of professors named João da Gama learned how to do it by reading instructions in a book he found in a mansion he bought in the Hawaiian island of Molokai."

"Are you being sarcastic? Are you joking? Whose book and what instructions? What kind of place is named Hawaii and Molokai? This is becoming absurd."

"It gets more absurd. Listen. The man who wrote the manual was Horacio Fuente, my father."

"But if your father got stuck in the past, and then wrote the instructions for his future self to use." He put his hands to his temples and moaned. "So, your father travels to the past with a spherical astrolabe. He cannot return because his astrolabe is damaged. He lives out a new life here and writes a book telling his story, including how the spherical astrolabe was converted into a time machine. Then someone in future discovers the book and travels to the past with his fellow professors, including your father. And the cycle begins again. Do I have that right?"

"That's partially right. My father charged me with the task of making sure his former colleagues in Hawaii would never use the astrolabe, or his book, to travel back in time." She could see that Afonso was becoming more befuddled. "Look, Afonso, I know you have more questions, but let's continue this discussion later. Right now, it's almost time for the muezzin's call to prayer. Let's go out on the pier."

The sky had not yet begun to lighten when the three of them reached the end of the pier. They were staring out into the ocean blackness for at least 10 minutes when Afonso said, "How much longer before we hear the call to prayer?" I'm getting cold."

Just then they heard the muezzin's voice float over the city loud and clear: *"Allahu Akbar. Ashhadu an la ilaha illa Allah!"*- Afonso said to the two cousins, "It means `God is most great. I bear witness that there is no god except the one God.'" Almost immediately after he said that, they heard three loud cannon booms coming from about a mile away.

Afonso was speechless, and so were Beatriz and Alessandra. They slowly walked back into the city. Before they parted Afonso said, "I believe you now. But that doesn't mean I have no more questions. You can expect me to pester you endlessly, so get ready." He turned down a street that would take him to his boats. The two cousins kept walking straight to their inn.

CHAPTER TWENTY-TWO

MORE QUESTIONS

A History Lesson

Afonso continued taking his dinner meals at the *Funduq Mendes* and peppering Alessandra and Beatriz with more questions. He decided he couldn't disprove Alessandra's story so he probed her for more information about Ahmad Grañ. She told him the same thing she had told Beatriz and Father Rodrigo. Afonso said, "I just cannot believe that the might of Portugal and truth of the Holy Church will disappear from the Horn of Africa in 45 years. Mogadishu, Malindi, Mozambique and Abyssinia all have Christian communities."

"Well, if the history of the Horn of Africa as my father knew it is the same history we shall experience, all will be swept away; and not only by Muslims. Abyssinia will not tolerate Portuguese Catholics after the early part of the 17th century, when it will expel them because of their priests' attempts to convert the Abyssinian people to Catholicism. If you doubt this, I suppose you could investigate Abyssinia's Orthodox Church by traveling there yourself and asking about that church's opinion of Catholicism."

"Wait. You just implied that the history your father knew might not be our history. If, as you say, your father traveled back in time from the future, then surely he would know what will happen here."

Alessandra look downcast for a moment then answered, "Just

recently I found his written explanation of that paradox. He wrote that when someone travels to the past with a modified spherical astrolabe, it's a different past than the one he had studied. He called it a `parallel past.' He discovered that difference almost as soon as he arrived here. Mogadishu—that is to say, Mogadishu's society, its people, its institutions—were not the same as described in the history books my father had studied."

"So, it might be possible that there won't be a regional war with the Portuguese supporting Abyssinia? Why would Portugal do that? Catholic Portuguese supporting an Orthodox kingdom makes no sense."

Alessandra sat back in her chair. They had taken seats in the common room after dinner. Alessandra said, "In my father's history books, the Portuguese were paid well to support the Abyssinian emperor against the attack by Grañ. Perhaps that will be their only motivation. Or perhaps the Portuguese king will hope to gain influence with the Abyssinian emperor, although I think he will only be interested in Abyssinia's gold."

Afonso sat silent for a few minutes. Beatriz joined them after the staff had finished cleaning up after dinner. Afonso turned to her and asked, "And what do you think of your cousin's theory?"

She looked at Alessandra then turned back to Afonso. "Oh, she just enjoys shocking people. I wouldn't pay any attention to her if I were you."

Afonso laughed and asked, "But you pay attention to her, don't you?"

"Well, I probably would be more skeptical if I hadn't grown up sitting around the fire upstairs listening to her father's stories."

Afonso turned again to Alessandra. "You say that your father believed his book would begin the next stage in its voyage to Hawaii; or is it Molokai?"

Alessandra said, "Molokai is one of eight major islands and several atolls that make up the state of Hawaii in the United States of

America. And yes, my father believed the book would end up there and would be found by his colleague at the University of Hawaii in 2018."

"Tell me again why he was so sure of the book's journey."

Beatriz answered him, "He was so sure because the book had set in motion his trip to the past. Look, we've gone over this mysterious time-travel loop already. I say we should take a walk in the glorious, moonlit evening. I'll tell you both the story of Grañ's widow who will bring the book to the ruler of Harar, in Abyssinia. That is, unless our history is not the same as Professor Horacio Fuente's history."

As they began walking through the Hamar Weyne neighborhood Alessandra said, "Beatriz, you said Grañ's widow would bring the book to Harar. Did my father tell you that? When I was still living at home, he told me that he wasn't sure what would happen to the book."

"Yes. That was his conclusion—that Grañ's widow, the Harari noblewoman Batíd-al Wambára, would take the book with her after the battle."

"Well, I don't know how sure he was of that. He knew from historical records that she would leave the main encampment after hearing of Grañ's death in the battle. I don't recall my dad telling us any more than that."

Beatriz said, "A few years later he told us that he had thought more about the aftermath of the battle. According to the historical record, Batíd-al Wambára would leave the main encampment with 300 horsemen and all of Grañ's many valuable possessions. She knew that her late husband was convinced the book was imbued with supernatural powers. Grañ wouldn't have left the book at camp instead of taking it to the battle with him. If she shared, or at least honored, Grañ's conviction, she would take the book with her."

Afonso interjected, "Now the story gets interesting!"

Beatriz said to Afonso, "Alessandra's father also told us that when Batíd-al Wambára remarries she will give Grañ's possessions to her new husband, Nur ibn Mujahid. He is, or will be, the Emir of Harar. Horacio told us the Emir was barely literate in Arabic and didn't read Portuguese either. Alessandra's dad also knew that the Emir would build a wall around Harar in 1550 and establish a madrasa there."

Afonso said, "That still doesn't settle the question of what will happen to the book."

Alessandra said, "I'm inclined to agree with my father's conclusions. I believe the book will end up in Harar, probably placed in that library.

Planning for Departure

Things became very busy at the Port of Mogadishu in the next few weeks. Ships of all kinds came into port, but mostly galleons and caravels. Business was brisk, goods were being offloaded and carted to warehouses, crews came into the city for a few days of rest and recreation. Then an interesting turn of events occurred. Afonso came in late one evening just after the staff had finished cleaning up after dinner. Beatriz welcomed him. "Why don't you get comfortable in the library. I'll fetch Alessandra and we'll join you shortly."

When they came into the library Afonso said, "I have some interesting news. I was with my crew at the docks just now unloading our catch when I met Captain Negasi Seyoum of the *Mythos*."

Alessandra said, "Oh, I know him. I was a passenger on the *Mythos* from the Port of Suez to here."

"Well, he did say he recently transported here a beautiful young female Portuguese professor."

"Oh, stop. He said no such thing. You're making it up."

"Actually, I'm not. He did mention transporting a woman here who was a professor. I did, however, make up the part that he said she was young."

Beatriz laughed and put her hand on Alessandra's arm. She looked at Afonso and said, "You'd better stop. I'm not sure I'll be able to keep my cousin from hitting you."

Alessandra extricated her arm and said, "I do hope you invited him here to dine while his caravel is being unloaded and loaded."

"Indeed, I did. He said he would be honored to join us for dinner tomorrow."

After Afonso left, Beatriz said, "You know, my dear. I think we should solicit Mr. Seyoum's advice on the fastest way to travel up to Zeila. When you said it took you six days on his caravel from Zeila to Mogadishu, and you described how tiny your cabin was, I thought I could never make a trip like that."

"Oh, when did you decide to accompany me to Zeila? I thought I would be going alone."

"I had decided that someone with common sense should accompany you."

"And when you couldn't think of anyone, you decided I would have to make do with you?"

Beatriz didn't know whether to laugh or get offended. "Anyway, once you described what it was like to travel on a caravel, I wasn't sure I could tolerate being uncomfortable for that long."

"Well, it wasn't that uncomfortable. Some nights I slept on deck, outside in the open air."

"But still, it must have been hot at night when you tried to sleep."

"The heat wasn't bad. Nor was I bothered much by the motion of the ship as it rose and fell."

Beatriz was silent for a moment and then said, "Have you thought of going overland?"

"Overland? Are you crazy? How, and what route?"

Beatriz winked and said, "I think I'll surprise you tomorrow."

They dropped the subject and went to bed. The next day was spent with preparations for the dinner that evening. They arranged for the dinner's main course to be anything but fish. They decided on lamb. They put out bottles of wine. After dinner they would serve a new beverage called *bunna*.

Negasi arrived as dinner guests were sitting in the common room adjacent to the dining room waiting for dinner to be served. Alessandra greeted him as he entered the lobby. "Welcome to my humble abode. I find it a great deal more comfortable than your caravel."

Negasi chuckled. "I don't doubt that." Looking around at the lobby he said, "I'm very impressed at the beauty of your inn. You did say it's your inn, if memory serves."

"Your memory is correct. And my cousin Beatriz is my co-owner. Here she is now." When Beatriz walked up to them, Alessandra did the introductions. "Captain, this is my cousin Beatriz Lopes. Beatriz, this is Captain Negasi Seyoum."

Beatriz said, "I'm very pleased to meet you. And thanks for bringing my cousin back home safely. By your name I guess you are Abyssinian."

"That's correct. I was born in Harar."

Alessandra smiled and said, "Ah, Harar. I've heard many interesting things about it. One thing I learned is the city is the birthplace of a wonderful beverage they call *bunna*. We here in Somalia have only in the past few years begun drinking it. But we use the Arabic name for it, *qahwah*."

Negasi nodded. "It has an interesting history. A popular legend in Abyssinia has the origin of the bean in Kaffa province, in the far southwest. According to the legend, a goatherd noticed his goats became very frisky after eating the leaves and berries of the bush. The goatherd ate some of the beans and his energy was restored.

"I suppose the Arabic word derives from the name of the province, perhaps because the word Kaffa was stamped on the bags that the dried beans were sold in. The people of Abyssinia call it *bunna*, but I'm afraid I don't know the origin of that name." At this point, a dining room staffer announced that dinner was ready to be served.

After dinner, the guests were served *qahwah* in small porcelain cups. First a waiter placed a small brazier of glowing charcoal on each table. On top of the brazier was placed a small pot of water. When the water was about to come to a boil, the waiter put several scoops of *qahwah* into the pot. After the water boiled for a few minutes, the dark brown qahwah was poured into each guest's cup. Bowls of small chunks of rock sugar were on the tables for the guests.

When they were finished, Beatriz and Alessandra showed Negasi around the inn. Upstairs, the large, hand-painted picture of Horn of Africa captivated him.

"This is a beautiful painting! Did your father paint this?"

Alessandra felt she had no choice but to provide Negasi an answer that was true but just a little disingenuous. "Yes, but he based it on a painting he had studied in his years as a professor. An Italian painter named Stefano Bonsignori painted the original painting for the Pope."

As Negasi examined the painting, Beatriz put her finger to her lips, winked at Alessandra and said, "Negasi, tell me what you think of this idea I have. Alessandra must return to Zeila soon to complete a task that she undertook. But she doesn't want to spend six or seven days, seasick, and trying to sleep in a cramped cabin.

"In our youth, from the ages 10 to 17, Alessandra and I were quite accomplished horseback riders. We even camped a few times along an inland river. I listened to one of our guests recently describe a trip he and a few companions made northeast, through the Ogaden region, to the Port of Zeila. They rode horseback, camping overnight along the way, and made the trip in three and a half days. The countryside was semi-arid highland country. There were small streams along the way interspersed about half a day's ride apart."

Negasi said, "If you're asking me whether I think such a trip is advisable, I would say maybe. It all depends on the time of year, your riding skills, how many riders would accompany you, and the political situation in that region. I'm sure you're aware that historically the Ogaden has been the subject of armed disputes between Abyssinia and Somalia."

Alessandra nodded, "I understand. But the Adal Sultanate controls the territory from the Port of Zeila to the city of Harar. At the present time, I am told there is no conflict with Abyssinia."

"I don't know how long that peace will last. Maybe a bigger obstacle would be the lack of water and grass for the horses. I would say a trip through the northern highlands would best be undertaken in May. That's when the light rainfall that began in March will have replenished the small streams by next month. There will also be sufficient grass and scrub for horses. But by the end of June the streams will have dried up and temperature will have risen to an uncomfortable degree. So, if you contemplate such a journey, you would be wise to begin soon."

Beatriz looked from Negasi to Alessandra. She said to no one in particular, "Well, it sounds like a fun trip to me!" She said to Alessandra, "If you're serious about going overland instead of by sea, I'm going with you."

Alessandra said, "But who will mind the inn if you and I both leave on this trip? There and back overland means seven to ten days away from the inn."

"As you know, we have a very competent staff. Our bookkeeper Manolo will be quite capable of handling the front desk. Luisa does a fine job overseeing the maids. Diogo has been in charge of the kitchen for years, and he won't need us to tell him how to do his job."

Negasi raised his hand and said, "I have an idea. I was going to mention this when you started talking about going horseback to Zeila. I just put my caravel in dry-dock for at least ten days. The hull is in bad shape and needs quite a few repairs. If you two are serious about making this trip on horseback, I would suggest we hire horses from one of Mogadishu's post rider companies."

Alessandra laughed and said, "You said 'we,' I heard you. Does this mean the esteemed owner of the *Mythos* is a horseman also?"

Negasi smiled and blushed. "Indeed I am. Or was. I was a horseman in my youth before I left Harar behind and headed for the sea. I rode on a fine Arabian gelding all the way here. I loved that horse. He was with me for another seven years before his heart gave out."

Beatriz clapped and laughed. "I can see us galloping along through the grassland, between mountains, and sleeping on the ground beside streams. But how risky would that be? When you and I, Alessandra, were girls we used to ride horses along the Shabelle and Juba rivers.

But we were not far from Mogadishu and other Somali cities. The trip we're contemplating would take us far from Somali cities and dangerously close to the frontier with Abyssinia. Do we need to worry about that?"

Negasi said, "As your cousin said, the frontier is peaceful at present. We can follow the Shabelle River from Mogadishu northeast as far as the Abyssinian highlands before the river veers to the northwest up into the highlands. From there, we would have to leave the river and continue heading northeast toward Zeila."

Alessandra said, "I have a question, Negasi. If you accompany us to Zeila, would you return with us a few days later? I mean, you said the *Mythos* would be in dry dock for at least 10 days."

"Yes, what I was thinking of was the three of us traveling together there and back. As for security, why don't I ask my Chief Engineer Ibrahim Hassan if he would like to accompany us. He also is familiar with the hinterlands thereabouts. He left his home in the Semien Mountains of Abyssinia. And he is an accomplished horseman. Two men and two women would be a slightly more formidable group. Especially since each man will be armed with an espingarda."

Alessandra was surprised. "Oh. Oh, I hadn't counted on the need to be armed. What's an espingarda?"

Beatriz looked at Alessandra with mock pity. "You've been gone too long, my dear cousin. It's a long firearm, a type of rifle. Some Arab traders from Malindi sell them here. I think it would be wise to be armed."

Alessandra laughed. "I don't mean to be rude, but are you going to be armed?"

"No, and you aren't either. The two gentlemen will be sufficient."

"Well, let's get ready! Negasi, you can ask Ibrahim if he would like to join us. And then find out about hiring horses. Beatriz and I will inform the staff of their additional responsibilities."

Last Minute Details

Alessandra was working in the office the next morning when she heard a knock on the office door. "Oh, welcome, Ibrahim. It's nice to see you again. I can see Negasi didn't waste any time! I hope you're here to tell us you can't wait to risk your life accompanying us poor defenseless women!"

"It's nice to see you again. And yes, I can't wait to risk my life on this horseback ride through Somalia."

Alessandra laughed. "I hope you're enjoying your time off. Although I don't know whether I believe you're here voluntarily."

"Oh, I assure you, it's quite voluntary. I haven't gone on a journey through the Ogaden in many years. I can't wait to revisit the land I crossed so long ago."

"Come on in and let's find you a room. I suspect our group won't be heading out to the bush until tomorrow at the earliest. Do you happen to know where your Captain is at the present moment?"

Before he could answer, Beatriz walked up. "And who is this handsome young gentleman?"

Alessandra said, "This is Ibrahim Hassan, Captain Seyoum's Chief Engineer aboard the *Mythos*. Ibrahim, this is my cousin and business partner, Beatriz Lopes."

"Pleased to meet you, Ibrahim. Alessandra has told me all about her voyage with you and Captain Seyoum."

Ibrahim smiled. "I'm very pleased to meet you, Miss Lopes. I look forward to our upcoming adventure."

"You can start calling me Beatriz now that we're about to spend a few weeks together. Follow me and I'll take you to your room. You can leave your things in the room and join the rest of the guests for lunch in an hour or so."

As Beatriz led Ibrahim to his room, Alessandra saw Negasi standing in the entrance to the inn. "Good morning, my friend. Your

Chief Engineer just arrived. Beatriz is showing him to his room. Why are you standing in the entrance?"

"We need to stable our horses but I don't know where your stables are."

Alessandra smiled and said, "Follow me. The stables are at the top of the U, on the other side of the fenced garden." As they stepped out of the entrance, she noticed the four horses being held by a young woman. "What beautiful animals! I see you chose palfrey geldings." She smiled at the young woman. "And what's your name, young lady?"

"Fatima. My parents own the *Rihlat Amina* stables, *Viagem Segura* in Portuguese."

Alessandra said, "I'll show you the stables." Turning to Negasi she said, "I take it these horses are post riders?"

"Yes, they can walk or trot all day. And they are not frightened by gunshot or wild animals, except for the cats of course. But we aren't likely to encounter cats. They would see or hear us and run away. Other harmless animals are plentiful, like baboons, giraffes, elephants, bush pigs and antelopes. We intend to do some hunting along the way. Dried beef and chicken will get tiresome after the first day."

"When I was young, I remember my mother bought a whole antelope from a local hunter. She and my father cut and cleaned it and preserved half of it with salt and spices. The six of us feasted on the rest."

"Well, I'm sure we'll manage to get an antelope. They graze in large herds; 40 or 50 animals. When we see a herd Ibrahim and I will ride far wide of them, double back, and hide in front of the herd. You and Beatriz can tie up your horses and start walking toward the rear of the herd. I'll get the first shot; if I miss, Ibrahim will take a shot."

"I take it the horses will find adequate grazing?"

"At this time of year, the land is full of grass and other plants. We'll probably see banana, papaya and guava trees as well."

"And I would guess we'll see shepherds and sheep along the way."

"Probably not many after we pass the curve of the river and continue on to the northeast. Most herdsmen don't stray far from the river."

When Fatima was satisfied with the horses' accommodations, Negasi paid her and she left. He and Alessandra walked back to the lobby. Ibrahim and a porter were just bringing in the rest of the equipment they would need on the trip. Piled just inside the entrance were four saddlebags, clothing, blankets, food, flints, knives, gunpowder, several bags of lead balls, a pouch full of silver and copper coins, and the two rifles. He said to Alessandra, "Beatriz tells me you two have gathered your belongings. Early in the morning, before dawn, we can load everything into our saddlebags and be off."

*   *   *

Alessandra was having trouble sleeping. She could hear Beatriz snoring in her bedroom, but that wasn't what was keeping her awake. After trying unsuccessfully to sleep for an hour, she got up, lit her desk lamp, and took another look at the forgeries she had prepared for replacing certain pages in her father's book. She planned to remove his drawing of a spherical astrolabe, remove all pages referring to an astrolabe, and remove the pages describing how her father grew up in Hawaii. In their place, she had composed a new history for him—the history he himself often told friends and colleagues:

"I was born in Sagres and lived there until my mother died when I was 10. My father took me with him to the Maghreb, in Northwest Africa. He was a shopkeeper, and I was his assistant. Most of the people there were the Berbers. Even though Arabic was not spoken much around the proud Berber people, my

father insisted I learn formal Arabic and put me into the local madrassa. As it turned out, I was very fortunate that he did that, because I learned my letters and mathematics. Since we were Portuguese and not Arabs, my father's business was moderately successful. When my father died, I sold his shop, travelled east and eventually made my way to Mogadishu."

Finally, she was satisfied she had done everything she could. *I have to assume this will be enough.* Just in case she had more ideas when she arrived, she brought several more sheets of paper, several pens, and an inkwell.

CHAPTER TWENTY-THREE

ZEILA ON HORSEBACK

Dawn Departure

Ibrahim and Negasi had the horses saddled before dawn. The two other members of the "Riders," as Beatriz decided they would call themselves, showed up a few minutes later, carrying the things they would put in the saddlebags. Negasi and Ibrahim were about to put the rifles in narrow leather scabbards when Beatriz said, "They look shorter than I remember seeing them in the firearm shops. Did you modify them?"

Ibrahim said, "No, they were already modified by local craftsmen. We wanted the shorter version of the espingarda because it will be strapped above the saddlebags aimed back to front."

Negasi said, "Strapped like this, Ibrahim and I will be able to pull them out of the scabbard quickly without having to dismount. They're loaded and ready to fire." Alessandra tried to hide her grimace.

When Beatriz finished stowing her gear in her saddlebags, she said, "Wow, I was worried the amount of stuff I'm bringing wouldn't fit in my saddlebags, but I'm pleasantly surprised. Alessandra, how are you doing with your packing?"

"No problem. I love how these horses are so calm while we're loading the saddlebags on their backs."

"They're used to carrying much more," said Negasi. "They're post carriers, remember."

Ibrahim walked around each horse and checked the saddles and stirrups. When he was satisfied, he said, "Well, it looks like we're ready to ride out. Beatriz, I suggest you lead, since you know the city better than Negasi and I. I'll ride behind you, Alessandra behind me, and Negasi at the rear. Once we're clear of the city and in open country, I'll take the lead since I know the countryside pretty well." With that, everyone mounted and urged their horses slowly forward out to the street. From there, they increased their pace gradually. The city was still asleep, except for the bakers who were pulling their loaves out of the ovens and setting them on cooling racks.

The city of Mogadishu sprawled out for several miles before following the Shabelle River to the northeast. Ibrahim rode to the front and switched places with Beatriz. Then he slowed, turned around in his saddle, and said, "We'll stay close to this side of the river for several hours. When it starts climbing to the left, it goes up into the Abyssinian highlands, all the way up to its source. We won't follow the river at that point. We'll continue riding northeast until we turn east and avoid the town of Beledweyne. After we've passed far to the east of the town, we'll double back straight north. The land starts to rise steadily. From there, as I recall, we'll ride through beautiful grassland for at least six or seven hours. We will look for a place to make our camp before it gets too dark. For the next two days after that, we'll see lots of grassland, small streams, and plentiful wildlife."

Day Two: North into the Ogaden

They found a suitable place to stop and make camp after the sun had sunk behind the low hills. The next morning, they rose early, ate a quick meal of wheat porridge and continued their ride north. They stopped after four hours to let the horses graze and drink from a small stream they were crossing. Alessandra shaded her eyes and pointed to movement in the distance. "What do you suppose that is, Negasi? I see some sort of flock and maybe some figures on horseback."

Negasi said, "Yes, I saw them just before we stopped. We should proceed slowly to avoid surprising them. They might be simple pastoralists. Or they might be pastoralists commissioned by the Ajuran Sultanate to keep watch over the border. If it's the latter, let me do the talking. If any of the rest of you is asked questions, do not speak Portuguese. Speak Arabic or Somaliña. I will give my name as Jamal. Alessandra, if you're asked for your name, you are Leila. Beatriz, you are Amina. Each of you should cover your head with a scarf."

The group set out again, this time very slowly. Eventually they were approached by a rider who had detached himself from the other two men watching over the flock of sheep. He was wearing the green colors of the Sultanate and was armed. He reined in his horse, withdrew his rifle and placed it across his saddle. "I must ask you your business and where you are headed." Pointing to Negasi he said, "What are your names?"

"My name is Jamal. This is my brother Ibrahim and my wives Leila and Amina. We are headed for Zeila."

The soldier looked at each of them and said to Negasi, "What is your business in Zeila?"

"My wife Leila's parents are buried at the *Masjid al-Qiblatayn*. We are going to pray for the progress of their souls."

The soldier looked skeptical. "I think you must be coming from Mogadishu. What is your business there?"

Ibrahim started to speak, but the soldier silenced him. "I am not asking you. I am asking your brother. Jamal, answer my question."

Negasi said, "I am first mate of the caravel *Mythos*. Ibrahim is chief engineer. Our captain ordered the ship put into dry dock for at least three weeks. My wives live in Mogadishu with my elderly mother. We decided to take advantage of the time to ride overland to Zeila."

The soldier seemed to run out of questions for the moment. Then there was a shout from the two other men watching the sheep. Negasi said, "It looks like some of the animals are looking for greener pasturage."

The soldier turned his horse around and said, "I must return. Go on your way and give my respects to Imam Abdullah."

The soldier rode back to assist in getting the flock together. Ibrahim smiled and said, "That was quick thinking on your part. Maybe we were lucky the soldier didn't question your `wives.'"

The rest of the day was uneventful. They made good progress across the vast grassland and a few rolling hills. Late that afternoon they stopped at a shaded small stream. They unsaddled and rubbed down the horses. Ibrahim said, "I'm going to follow this stream and see if I can find an unsuspecting animal that I can invite to join us for dinner."

Beatriz nodded and said to the others, "Let's lay out our bedrolls and find some dry kindling in case our noble hunter comes back with something to cook."

Alessandra and Negasi returned with armloads of firewood just as a shot rang out nearby. Negasi grabbed his rifle and ran off in the direction of the shot. An hour passed and Beatriz said, "I hope they're okay." As they waited, they made a small fire to cook some porridge.

Another half hour passed, and then Ibrahim and Negasi came walking up carrying a small antelope draped on a long tree branch. The animal had been gutted and cleaned. Negasi said, "That fire needs to be a lot bigger. Dinner's on its way."

Ibrahim said, "I got in a lucky shot while the poor creature was having a drink at the stream. I said a *mitzvah* blessing before I began gutting it. Negasi walked up just in time to help me."

Alessandra and Negasi cleaned and cut the small antelope up into quarters. Beatriz took one of the quarters and cut it into smaller pieces. Ibrahim came up after having washed his hands, cut up another quarter into smaller pieces, and began skewering pieces for cooking over the fire.

While the meat was cooking, Negasi started a pot of water boiling for tea. Beatriz took out salt from a pouch in one of the saddlebags. "It looks like we'll have more than enough meat for the rest of the journey."

As the afternoon turned into evening, the four travelers sat around the fire. Negasi stared through the flames and into the darkness. He saw the ancestors facing him, concerned, yet confident. Ibrahim turned to Alessandra and said, "You know, I just realized I don't know what your business is in Zeila. Does it have something to do with the Zeila mosque you visited on our way down to Mogadishu?"

"Yes, it does. The package I carried to the mosque contained a book written by my father. He had wanted me to ask the Imam to preserve it for him in the mosque archive."

"The *Masjid al-Qiblatayn* is well known for its library, school and archives. If I'm not being too nosy, may I ask why your father wanted his book deposited in a mosque archive? Does the book have something to do with Islam?"

Beatriz was chewing on her bottom lip as she looked across the campfire at Alessandra. Negasi also was watching Alessandra intently. She sighed and said, "You know, Ibrahim, and you, Negasi. By now I consider you friends. And as Beatriz knows, I am tired of lying to people about my father."

Ibrahim said, "Alessandra, Negasi and I assure you that whatever you tell us about your father will go no further."

Alessandra said, "Well, his story is quite unusual, I assure you." Looking at Beatriz and chuckling, she continued, "I told this story to Afonso back in January, but it took quite a while for him to believe me. It wasn't until gave him some proof that he finally succumbed to my unusual tale. Of course, out here in the Ogaden wilderness I won't be able to produce the proof that satisfied Afonso. But I can show you the proof when we return."

Beatriz said, "Alessandra, I suggest you start with the near future before we depart for the distant future."

Her comment surprised the two men. Ibrahim smiled and said, "That's fine. What's going to occur in the near future?"

Alessandra said, "I don't know if you consider 18 years near enough, but here it is. The Adal Sultanate in Zeila will lapse into anarchy after the governor of Zeila is killed during a campaign against Abyssinia."

Negasi said, "I'm not going to ask how you know this yet. I want to hear the rest of the story, especially the part about your father. Proceed, and pardon my interruption. I'll pour you a cup of tea."

He stood, poured a cup and handed it to Alessandra. She continued, "After the death of the governor a great warrior will take control of Zeila and Harar in 1520. He will invade Abyssinia nine years later, and with the help of Ottoman weapons, conquer most of the country. He will be killed in 1543 and the total conquest of Abyssinia will be averted."

Ibrahim asked, "Can you tell us the name of this great warrior who will arise?"

"He is known by two names: Imam Grañ and Ahmad Grañ."

He and Negasi frowned. Negasi said, "The name `Grañ' is not a Somali or Arabic name. It's the Amharic word `Left-handed'. Why would a Somali warrior call himself `Left-handed'?"

Alessandra said, "The Abyssinians will call him that after seeing him fight with his left hand."

There was silence. Silence punctuated by the sound of crickets and the hissing of the dying fire. She continued after taking a sip of her tea. "Now, before I continue on to my father's story, let me say that these events I just described may not take place. My father had studied the history of this region in his professional life, and these facts I'm telling you are facts from the history my father studied.

"But a strange thing happened when my father traveled back in time to Mogadishu in 1430." She paused to sip her tea and awaited the inevitable explosion of questions.

Negasi and Ibrahim practically spoke at once. Ibrahim said, "I expect you want to delay explaining the part of your father's voyage to the past so that you can proceed with the events in the near future."

"No, actually, the story of how my father came to Mogadishu is fairly simple, relative to what he discovered about time travel. He traveled here using a time machine created from a spherical astrolabe. He was part of a group of academic colleagues who wanted to study Mogadishu. But the group had to return to 2019 abruptly to avoid being taken prisoner by the Chinese Admiral Zheng He, whose fleet was in port. All of them made it back to the future except my father. The spherical astrolabe he was using broke when he fell while running from the marketplace."

Again, there was silence except for the sound of crickets. Then Negasi said, "You say you have proof. I for one would like to see your proof. That's not to say I disbelieve your story; just that I would enjoy seeing what you have."

"Well, here is the strange fact that surprised my father and makes the events I have just told you merely probable, not definite. He discovered that the Mogadishu he had studied in his career as a history professor at the University of Hawaii was different from the history he landed in, so to speak."

Ibrahim asked, "What was the difference?"

"The history literature my father had studied and written about in his career described this whole region as being a great deal less diverse than it is as we know it. For example, there were no Catholic churches, no Portuguese community, no Jewish community, no fleets of caravels captained by anyone other than Arabs and Indians. Even the university I attended and worked at, the University of Padua, had no women students or professors for hundreds of years in my father's world."

Ibrahim asked, "As if time travel were not strange in itself, it sounds like your father traveled back to a different world."

"That's what he concluded. He described this world, our world, as occupying what he called a `parallel dimension.' What he meant was, as far as I understand, history isn't merely one train of events on a single track. It's more than one, and any event that occurs on one track may or may not occur on the other track in the same way. That is why he emphasized to me that the events I just described to you about the near future may not occur."

Negasi turned to Beatriz and asked, "Have you seen the evidence your cousin is talking about?"

"Yes, I have. Her father showed those things to us. And Alessandra's mother described Horacio's arrival." She stood and began pouring water on the hot ashes of the fire. "Well, my friends, as Horacio Aleixandre Fuente was fond of saying, let's sleep on it."

Day Three: More Questions

Before dawn the next morning, they ate some more of the meat, accompanied by cold porridge and cold tea. Ibrahim walked over to a nearby papaya tree and picked several fruits. He handed them out to the others and said, "Peel them and crush the fruit. Then mix the pulp with salt and rub the mixture into the meat. We can wrap the meat in the papaya skins and some cloth for the day's journey. When we stop for the night, we can wash the salt off the pieces we plan to eat. The papaya pulp and skins will tenderize the meat somewhat."

The horses were restless to get moving, having been hobbled and tied to a nearby tree all night. The friends mounted and continued on their journey. After a few hours Alessandra said to her cousin, "I don't know about you but horseback riding is no longer fun."

"I agree. Did you notice I almost fell dismounting yesterday? My old legs are out of shape."

"I'm hoping we might find a southbound caravel we can get on for the trip home."

They rode in four-hour stages, dismounting to stretch and to let the horses graze on the plentiful grass and drink from streams. For the rest of the day, they saw only unending fields of grass and brush. Finally, they stopped to make camp in a small group of trees. They tied the horses with long ropes to give them more grazing space, and rubbed them down.

Negasi said, "Tomorrow, about midafternoon, we should be well past the last of the hills. The owner of the post horses told me to expect to see elephants between those hills and the coast. We should stay well away from them. We may also see lions, but they will not bother us. The meat we have will sustain us for the rest of our journey. I think we shall reach the city before dusk."

Beatriz asked Negasi, "Are you familiar with Zeila?"

"I am not. Each time our caravel docked at Zeila, I had to stay with the ship to oversee the unloading and loading. Ibrahim is fairly familiar with the city."

"Yes, I have explored it many times. I know where we return our horses."

As they made a fire, unwrapped and washed one of the antelope haunches, and spread out their bedding, the inevitable questions began. Negasi turned to Beatriz and asked, "So, you spent many years with Alessandra and her parents, is that right?"

"Actually, I spent more time with Alessandra's parents than she did. She left to attend the University when she was 20, and didn't return to Mogadishu for 40 years. Horacio used to talk about his past life in Hawaii from time to time. But most of the time, he enjoyed his life in Mogadishu married to Mariana, living with my parents and me, and working with his clients."

Negasi spitted the haunch and placed it on the fire. "Tell us about this place called Hawaii."

"Hawaii is a group of islands and atolls in the Pacific Ocean that make up the state of Hawaii in the United States of America. My father was born in Molokai, one of the islands, in 1953. Hawaii is one of 50 states in the United States of America. America is the name given to the continent discovered by Cristobal Colon seven years ago. You probably have heard of that voyage. Actually, the word 'America' is a corruption of the name of Amerigo Vespucci, the man who was thought to have drawn the map."

Ibrahim said, "Before you continue, let's take the meat and water off the fire. We can eat and drink our tea while you go on with the story." He took the antelope haunch off the fire, and Beatriz cut it into four pieces. Negasi took the boiling water off the fire and poured it on some tea leaves in a pitcher. Ibrahim said, "This device you say brought your father here, can you describe it?"

"Have you heard of a spherical astrolabe?"

Negasi said, "I have heard of it, but I've also heard that only the Portuguese mariners have them."

Alessandra laughed. "They were extremely hard to obtain. Even Vasco da Gama couldn't get one for his trip around the Cape of Good Hope last January. But my father had one, which was the broken time machine. By the 21st century they were considered collectors' items, decorative things only. They were no longer used as navigational devices. There were much more sophisticated navigational devices in the 21st century.

"He gave it to me and asked me to give it to Vasco da Gama when his fleet anchored off of Mogadishu on January 2. I did that and the Captain graciously accepted it. Father Rodrigo joined da Gama's ship as chaplain."

Negasi asked, "I've heard about a globe-shaped maritime navigational device with many wires and arrows indicating directions. Is that what you're talking about?"

"That's right. The group my father was a member of was called the `Starlight Commune.' They had obtained several and learned how to modify them so that they became time machines."

Ibrahim asked, "Are you saying da Gama's ships visited Mogadishu?"

"Not quite. They were worried the city would be hostile to Christians, as so many other African cities were. Except for Malindi, which is where they were headed on the way home from India."

Ibrahim laughed and said, "So now the Great Navigator has a time machine! I wonder where he will travel to next."

Everyone laughed at that, even Alessandra. "I'm sure he would try that if he understood the modification to the astrolabe. But the machine was broken. One of the silver wires that passed through the golden globe in the middle had broken inside the globe. My father said he had tried to find someone in Mogadishu who could extract the wire and repair it, but was told it was impossible."

Beatriz looked at the dying campfire and stood up. "Let's continue this conversation tomorrow. In Zeila! For now, let's put this fire out and put the meat back into its wrapping."

Day Four: Elephants!

As before, they broke camp and rode off well before dawn. It had rained lightly during the night but they were covered by canvas and didn't get wet. After about three hours angling up to the northeast, they halted suddenly at Ibrahim's raised-arm signal. As the others drew up next to him, they saw a family group of elephants in the distance. "It looks like there are six. I don't see any males, unless some of the smaller ones are males. The largest one on the left is probably the matriarch. We must proceed cautiously. Let's stop here, let the horses graze and drink, and we can observe the elephants' movements."

Beatriz asked, "Have you seen elephants before? It sounds like you have. But when?"

"Many years ago. As I told Alessandra last summer on Negasi's caravel, when I was young, I came to Zeila overland from Begemdir, in the Semien Mountains. It was a trip of more than a month on horseback. I saw many elephants as I passed through these grasslands."

Alessandra said, "I wanted to ask you more about the condition of Jews in that region. You said you left because you didn't want to be drawn into any of the battles with the Christian kingdom."

"Yes, that's right. My family and many others had fled the mountainous villages near Debarq and settled in the Begemdir region, where I was born. But even that city was plagued with periodic battles with the Abyssinian Christians. During a lengthy period when there was no violence on the roads, I rode out with just my horse and saddlebags. I was fortunate to have found work in as a longshoreman in Djibouti, and later being hired by Negasi on his caravel."

Beatriz said, "Hey, it looks like the elephants are moving away. They're going in a southerly direction. Will we be able to avoid them the way we're traveling?"

Ibrahim said, "Yes. We're fortunate they won't be in our way. And judging from how calm the matriarch is, we probably won't encounter any lions. Not that a lion would be a threat to the elephants."

The party mounted their horses and continued northeast. After they passed the extensive grasslands the ground became wetter and the sky became overcast. Soon they were riding to the east of a range of small hills. At that point, Ibrahim turned straight north. He slowed so he could ride alongside the others and said, "This range of hills marches straight to the Bay of Zeila." He rode forward again to lead the group.

After about three hours, they began to see small settlements, groups of three or four basket-shaped dwellings surrounded by a fence made of thorn branches. They could see goats grazing amongst the dwellings.

When they smelled the salt air of the sea Ibrahim said, "We're getting close to the outskirts of the city. When we enter the city proper, I'll lead us to the stables where we can leave the horses."

CHAPTER TWENTY-FOUR

THE BOOK IS REBORN

A Surprise at the Pier

They left their stalwart horses at the *Iistablat Sahili*. Negasi told the owner, "We might want these very horses for the return trip to Mogadishu, but we're not certain we'll return on horseback." The owner agreed to hold them ready for a few days.

Alessandra said to Negasi as they walked away from the stable, "I heard you say we might not ride back to Mogadishu. What are you thinking?"

Beatriz said, "Yes, what's on your mind?"

Ibrahim chuckled and said to the women, "We hadn't mentioned our plan because we weren't sure it would come to fruition."

Negasi said, "When we left our ship in dry dock, we arranged for our crewmen to sail it back here to Zeila so we could ride back to Mogadishu on board a ship instead of on horseback. The trip by sea is twice as long, but I think we can all agree it would be twice as enjoyable."

Ibrahim said to the group, "The first thing we need to do now is see about accommodations for the night."

Negasi said to Alessandra, "I don't know how long it might be before the *Mythos* will arrive. It all depends on how long it takes to repair the hull in dry dock. In the meantime, Ibrahim and I will walk to the port and make inquiries. How much time do you anticipate your meeting with the Imam will take?"

"I really don't know. This is Friday, so it wouldn't be a good idea for me to interrupt the *salat al-jumu'ah* service after sunset. Tomorrow morning would be a good time to pay Imam Abdullah a visit."

It was a pleasantly warm afternoon as they walked to the nearby coach stand and hired one to take them and their bags into the center of the city. They found a very attractive inn not far from the port and deposited their saddlebags in their rooms. Alessandra removed her shoulder bag from her saddlebag. The proprietor of the inn told them the evening meal would be served in four hours.

Ibrahim said, "I suggest we walk around a bit to restore the blood to our legs." There were no objections, so they headed out towards the port. They were pleasantly surprised to see the *Mythos* just outside the first jetty, sails down and rowers bringing the ship into the harbor.

Negasi said, "Well, I call that very fortunate. Ibrahim and I will meet the ship at the dock. Beatriz and Alessandra don't have to come unless you want to."

Beatriz looked at Alessandra, who shook her head and answered Negasi. "I think I would like to go to the mosque and retrieve my father's book now. It's still early yet, and the evening service won't have started yet. Beatriz can stay and join you on board if she wants to."

Beatriz said to Alessandra, "I would like to come with you to the mosque. But let's stay and watch the docking for a few minutes."

The four of them stood on the pier and watched the crew on board guide the ship beside the end of the pier and secure it. Negasi and Ibrahim greeted the crew and joined them in securing the ship to the dock. Once the gangplank joined the ship to the dock, Negasi and Ibrahim boarded. Negasi went to find the captain. Ibrahim turned back and said to the women, "Are you sure you won't come on board to see what condition the cabins are in?"

Negasi rejoined them and said, "Well, the captain tells me the condition of ship's hull wasn't as bad as I had anticipated, just encrusted with barnacles. The ship brought passengers as well as cargo."

Beatriz said, "I think we'd rather not board until the cabins are restored to a condition fit for ladies!"

Negasi laughed and said, "That's fine. We have work to do here anyway. Go about your business and we'll see you at dinner."

Stevedores began unloading cargo as the three passengers emerged from their cabins and descended the gangplank. Alessandra and Beatriz walked away toward the center of town.

Expert Forgery

As they walked, Beatriz asked, "What exactly will you have to do to the book? You said you would make some corrections."

"I have to remove several pages and replace them with pages I have written." She smiled and added, "I'm an expert forger. I have also prepared a rectangular piece of finished black leather that will be glued onto the existing linen front and back covers. I've embossed some of my expert artwork to the front cover."

"If you need me to judge your forgeries and artwork, let me know. Otherwise, I'll just watch."

"You'll do more than just watch. We'll be ruining our fingernails untying the tiny little knots that hold the pages together."

When they approached the *Masjid al-Qiblatayn*, Beatriz said, "That is such a beautiful mosque! Much grander than the ones in Mogadishu." They stopped at the fountain next to the front door, took off their shoes, washed their feet and slipped on visitors' sandals. They covered their heads with scarves and entered. Alessandra was once again overwhelmed by the mosque's beauty. Beatriz was speechless for a few minutes. They walked slowly through the prayer hall. Beatriz looked down at the many carpets covering the room. On an impulse, she knelt down, facing the *mihrab*, and put her forehead to the carpet. Alessandra realized she had not had a chance to do that when she first visited the mosque. She knelt beside Beatriz, touched her forehead to the carpet, and mumbled a modest prayer for good fortune for herself and her country.

"Ahlaan biqa!" Imam Abdullah was smiling broadly as he walked up to them. The women stood and smiled.

Alessandra said, "Thank you. I promised you I would come back and pay you a visit. This lady next to me is my cousin, Beatriz Lopes."

"I'm very pleased to meet you. You and Alessandra brighten this mosque with your presence. Come, let's go into my office. May I offer you something? Tea?"

Alessandra smiled and said, "That would be lovely."

When the Imam returned with the tea, Alessandra said, "Imam Abdullah, my cousin and I decided to do some traveling and traveled here on our friend's caravel, the *Mythos*. While we are in port as cargo is delivered and loaded, I decided I would show my cousin my father's book. May we go to the archive and show Beatriz how magnificent it is?"

The Imam smiled. "It would be my pleasure." When they finished their tea, the Imam led them into the archive.

Beatriz exclaimed, "Oh, how wonderful! Our inn has a library but nothing so magnificent as this! Where is my uncle's book?"

Imam Abdullah walked to the back, removed the book from the shelf and handed it to Alessandra. "Would you like some privacy while you look through it? I have some work to do preparing for the evening service."

Alessandra smiled and nodded. She and Beatriz sat down at the table as the Imam left the room. Alessandra removed the oilcloth wrapping and set the book down. Then she took out her carefully forged pages and set them on the table beside the book.

Beatriz picked the forgeries up and glanced through them. She set them down and asked, "Where will you begin?"

"First I need to replace my father's description of his early life in Hawaii with a fictitious early life in Portugal. Here's what I wrote. `I was born in Sagres and lived there until my mother died when I was 10. My father took me with him to the Maghreb, in Northwest Africa. He was a shopkeeper, and I was his assistant. Most of the people there were the Berbers. Even though Arabic was not spoken much around the proud Berber people, my father insisted I learn formal Arabic and put me into the local madrassa. As it turned out, I was very fortunate that he did that, because I learned my letters and mathematics. Since we were Portuguese and not Arabs, my father's business was moderately successful. When my father died, I sold his shop, travelled east and eventually made my way to Mogadishu.'"

"Now read what he wrote in his book. Tell me what you think." Beatriz read the offending passage describing Horacio's life in Hawaii. Alessandra asked, "Well? Is mine adequate?"

"Adequate! It's more than adequate. And your forged handwriting looks exactly like his."

Alessandra smiled. "Now comes the difficult part. The original must be removed and replaced with this. As you can see, groups of ten pages are held together with a chain stitch using waxed linen thread."

"I see the knots at the end of each stitch. Boy, those are going to be difficult to untie!"

It took them almost 10 minutes to untie and remove the original page and replace it with the forgery. "Now let's do the same with the title page. My dad had written: `From the future to the past, by Dr. Horacio Fuente, retired professor of Near East History, University of Hawaii.'" Beatriz untied the thread and removed the title page. Alessandra replaced it with her forged page: "From Portugal to Mogadishu, by Horacio Fuente, retired notary and scribe."

Beatriz said, "Here's your father's drawing of the spherical astrolabe and his instructions on how to modify it."

"I'll just leave the drawing but replace the instructions with a description of how he obtained the device and what he did with it. Here's what I wrote:

"'In my career as notary, scribe and business consultant, I was fortunate to have obtained an extremely rare marine navigation device—a spherical astrolabe—from a retired owner of a fishing company. He had salvaged the device from an Indian caravel that had broken up on the rocks off shore from Mozambique. I recognized its value as a radical improvement on the traditional astrolabe. When my daughter Alessandra learned that the fleet of Vasco da Gama was anchored offshore, she had a fishing boat take her there, and she presented the astrolabe to the Captain.'"

Beatriz nodded and continued leafing through the book. "Your dad wrote beautifully throughout the book. I especially like how lovingly he wrote of meeting your mom and eventually marrying. In fact, everything he wrote about his life in Mogadishu is fine. Obviously, his description of the Starlight Commune, its genesis and membership, has to be removed. I'm eager to read what you've written."

"Mostly I'm just going to remove everything about Hawaii and the Starlight Commune. I've expanded on his life in Mogadishu to take its place." She and Beatriz carefully removed the offending pages and replaced them with Alessandra's beautiful forgeries.

"The next thing I'll do is remove what I wrote after the final page:

> "'I Alessandra Fuente tell you this:
> My father has dedicated this book to you.
> You who will travel back in time
> to the city of my parents' prosperity,
> to the city of my birth, Mogadishu.
> You will learn of my work in astronomy,
> before Copernicus and Galileo.
> Your voyage made our work possible.
> You who read this book
> must not attempt a subsequent journey.
> Do not return to rescue my father,
> your colleague, Horacio Fuente.
> Heed our plea and be content.
> You have accomplished much.'"

Alessandra then took out from her shoulder bag the black leather book cover she had made for the book. "Here's what I've prepared. This is the word `Grañ' written in Arabic, عراني and Amharic ግራኝ." The words, one above the other, were embossed on the finished outside of the book cover. She spread out the leather cover on the table and carefully set the book in the middle, spine down, to make sure it fit. "What we'll do is glue the leather cover onto the heavy linen covers."

Alessandra took out a bottle of glue from her bag and applied a coat over the entire inside surface of the leather. Beatriz placed the book upright on the glued surface, and Alessandra carefully covered the outside of the book with the leather cover. When they were finished, Alessandra wrapped the book in the oilcloth. They stood, stretched and walked to the Imam's office. Handing the book to him she said, "Imam Abdullah, thank you so very much for taking the time to allow me to show my father's book to my cousin. We'll be on our way now, but I hope to pay you another visit before too long."

She and Beatriz left the mosque and walked slowly back to their inn.

The Voyage Home

It was early June when the *Mythos* departed Zeila and began its journey south. The rainy season was still asserting its presence, so the cousins spent more time in their cabins than they had hoped. But after three days, the sun banished the rain clouds from the sky and proceeded to bake everyone on board the caravel.

At dawn on the seventh day the ship docked and the two passengers stepped onto the Mogadishu pier. Negasi said, "Once my crew has finished unloading cargo, the ship will need to remain docked for an inspection to ensure seaworthiness for the next voyage. May Ibrahim and I join you two at the inn for dinner?"

"Certainly. And bring along some of that Venetian glassware I noticed you had loaded in Zeila."

Negasi smiled. "Of course. It came from Istanbul. You can purchase them or I will take them back to the ship with me tonight."

Alessandra asked, "Istanbul? Does the shipment indicate the merchant in Istanbul?"

"Yes, the crate is stamped 'Marco Caratto, fine Venetian glassware from Angelo Barovier of Murano.' Is that someone you know?"

"Indeed, it is! I traveled with the young man from Venice to Alexandria. In fact, if memory serves, I advised him to set up his import business in Istanbul rather than Alexandria. I guess he took my advice. So yes, I think I might be interested in purchasing some to display."

Friendships Blossom

The cousins were ecstatic at being home again and dove right back into their work at the *Funduq Mendes*. Negasi and Ibrahim stayed at the inn every time they were in port. Afonso often took his meals there. During one quiet evening in the lounge after dinner, all three men were enjoying coffee and conversation with Beatriz and Alessandra. It was early December 1499. During a lull, Beatriz looked at Alessandra and said, "I wonder, dear, whether this might be a good time to bring up that subject we were discussing last night."

Ibrahim set his cup down and asked, "And what subject would that be, ladies?"

Alessandra set her cup down. "I think you all remember what I told you about my father's belief, based on what he knew of the history of the Horn of Africa, that this region would erupt in violence and anarchy sometime in the early years of the 16th century."

Negasi said, "Yes, but didn't you say that the history that he knew was not necessarily the history that will come to pass in our—what did you call it— parallel dimension?"

"Yes, that's right. There was no guarantee that events that he studied in his career would occur in our world. But they might occur."

Beatriz said, "What we're going to suggest is that we consider moving from Mogadishu to somewhere safe."

This comment resulted in complete silence for a few moments, complete save the noises of the kitchen crew cleaning up. Ibrahim was first to speak. "Can you give us examples of what the history books said happened in the Horn of Africa?"

"War with Abyssinia, killings of Zeila's rulers and elites, anarchy throughout the region. But, of course, in my father's world there was no significant population of Christians and Jews. And there were certainly no Portuguese."

Negasi asked, "Where would be somewhere safe in the Horn of Africa?"

"Maybe further south, but probably not. An idea occurred to me when you told me the name stamped on the crate of Venetian glassware. Marco Caratto was one of my traveling companions from Venice to Alexandria. I had advised him to consider setting up his business in Istanbul rather than Alexandria or Cairo. Apparently, that's what he did."

Ibrahim asked, "Are you implying that Istanbul would be any more peaceful, especially for Jews or Orthodox Christians?"

"I certainly am. Soon after the Spanish monarchs, Queen Isabela and King Ferdinand, united their kingdoms seven years ago, they ordered the Jews to either leave or convert to Christianity. When the Ottomans learned of this, the Sultan invited the Jews to come to Turkey."

Negasi said, "That's news to me. I wasn't aware that the Sultan was friendly toward Jews, or Christians for that matter. Muslims have been very hostile to Jews and Christians in Abyssinia. Is this `news' something that your father told you?"

"Well, yes and no. This event was frequently written about in his time. But I guess I hear more news from my guests than you do on board your ship. More than once in the past several months businessmen have passed along news of the upheaval in Spain and the Sultan's invitation. Turkey, Istanbul in particular, desperately needs to build up its professional class—businessmen, scholars, lawyers, artisans, and so forth. Turkish society is sorely lacking in those fields. And many of the Spanish Jews possess those skills."

"But you haven't said anything about Christians. Did the Sultan's invitation extend to Orthodox Christians?"

"Yes, Istanbul formerly had a large population of Greek Orthodox Christians. But that population was decimated by the war with the Ottoman Turks. I should think an Orthodox Christian from a different religious tradition would be welcomed."

Afonso said, "Well, if I may interrupt. I recall you saying that in a hundred years or so the Abyssinians would expel the Portuguese. I would think the Portuguese would be expelled from Somalia as well after the rise of this warlord you spoke of. And since the Mediterranean is a battleground between Portuguese and all other naval forces, it would appear the only safe place for a Portuguese person would be in Portugal itself. Would you agree?"

Alessandra smiled at Beatriz and said, "Here's where the situation gets interesting. When my cousin and I first started thinking about leaving this wonderful city for Istanbul, we were worried that we would be barred as Portuguese Catholics. Then I recalled a conversation I heard when I was young. I remember clearly how embarrassed my mother was when my father laughingly told her that her family name, Mendes, was a common name among Portuguese Jews. My mother admitted that her parents had told her that they were `conversos,' Jews who had undergone baptism and became Catholic."

Beatriz added, "Yes, I was there when we were all talking about that. My father then admitted that his surname, `Lopes,' was a Jewish name. My grandparents, and Alessandra's grandparents, were born

Jewish! That was one reason why they ultimately decided to leave Portugal years ago. They could already see how bad things were getting for Jews on the Iberian Peninsula. Even conversos were treated badly."

Alessandra turned to Afonso. "Now, dear Afonso. You probably believe you have `pure' Christian blood. Well, I have some sad news for you; or happy news, your choice. The surname `Escobar' is a name commonly adopted by Spanish and Portuguese Jews to avoid discrimination. So, my point is that you, just like Beatriz and myself, would be safe in proclaiming your Jewish ancestry to the Turkish immigration authorities. Otherwise, Portugal would be your only safe haven after 1520 or thereabouts."

Everyone was silent for a few moments. Then Ibrahim said, "What I'm going to say may come as a surprise, or it may not. Captain Negasi Seyoum and his Chief Engineer Ibrahim Hassan recently discussed what our plans might be in the near future. We're both in our mid-sixties. Perhaps the Good Ship *Mythos* should make one last trip up the Red Sea under the helm of Captain Seyoum."

Beatriz smiled. "Perhaps you would like to take the rest of us as passengers!"

Alessandra said to Beatriz, "Well, that would depend on how soon you and I could sell our inn. And then there is the question of room on the *Mythos* for all of us. There are only three cabins and five of us. But if two persons shared a cabin, there would be room for all five us." She looked at Beatriz and smiled.

Afonso said, "Let's slow down here. There are many things to consider. Like my little fishing fleet, for example. It would take time to sell the business."

Negasi said, "There's no rush. The *Mythos* has one more trip to make up to Suez and back. Let's talk more when we return. I think next year, perhaps the summer of 1500 would be a good target date. The distance from Alexandria to Istanbul is about a week by sea."

CHAPTER TWENTY-FIVE

NEW IDENTITIES

It was a little past noon when the five friends disembarked from the *Sant Andreu*, a very tall Catalan *Nave*. It docked where Istanbul's Golden Horn estuary met the Bosporus Strait. After the friends deposited their luggage at the shipping office, Afonso said, "I'm very tired of being on ships. No offense, Negasi. I loved your caravel. It was the best I've ridden on, and I've ridden on many, as you know."

"I miss it already, my friend. But I am also too old to be a ship's captain. And Ibrahim and I are very pleased at how much the *Mythos* sold for. The new owners are merchants I got to know in Suez."

Alessandra said, "I didn't know Ibrahim had an ownership interest in the *Mythos*. When did that happen?"

Ibrahim laughed. "From one point of view it happened 10 years ago. From another point of view, it happened one year ago." Alessandra looked over at Beatriz and smiled.

Ibrahim asked, "You two must have sold *Funduq Mendes* for a lot."

Beatriz chuckled. "You know exactly how much we sold it for. And Afonso's fishing company. Or have you forgotten we all pooled the proceeds and deposited them with the *khawala* merchant network when we arrived in Suez? That network, might I remind you, includes a prominent Marrano trading company in Istanbul. We won't have any trouble withdrawing all or part of our money."

Looking at Negasi, Ibrahim said, "Have you thought about us

maybe purchasing a building or a property with Afonso and these two ladies?"

"Yes, it did occur to me. But are we sure that Jews are allowed to own property in Istanbul?"

Alessandra said, "I think this early in the immigration flow from Spain, the Ottomans would welcome the investment. The Turkish population still hasn't recovered from the war with the Byzantines who controlled this land.

"And as I said when we first discussed this last December, the Ottomans might welcome a non-Greek Orthodox Christian, such as one from Abyssinia."

Negasi smiled. "Well, allow me to share a family secret. I'm just as Jewish as the rest of you! My father's family loved to talk about their legendary Jewish past. According to my grandfather, the family adopted the name Seyoum because their original surname, Semyen, was recognized as Jewish in the region they lived in. So, I too, have Jewish ancestry."

The five friends had continued walking as they talked. It felt wonderful to be walking. They had been stopping periodically to stretch as they made their way toward the immigration building.

Beatriz asked, "Is anyone worried that our claim to be Jewish might be rejected."

Alessandra replied, "No reason to worry. Remember what I said—the Ottoman government is going out of its way to welcome the Sefardi Jews of Spain and won't question their claims."

Alessandra was right. The immigration process took less than half a day, consisting of little more than signing a declaration. Negasi had decided to declare himself Jewish to be safe. When they were finished, they found themselves walking through the "Balat" Jewish quarter on the west bank of the Golden Horn.

Negasi said, "My business associate in Suez, the man who bought the *Mythos*, a Jew himself, told us to proceed directly to the Ahrida Synagogue. It was built about 65 years ago by the Romaniote Jews."

Turning to Ibrahim he asked, "Do you know anything about the difference between the Sefardi and the Romaniote?"

"Only that the latter have been in Turkey since the time of Christ. The Sefardi are Jews escaping the terror of Spain that began eight years ago."

Negasi smiled and said to the others, "Ask him what kind of Jew he is."

Ibrahim said, "Negasi wants you to believe that merely because he started studying Judaism a few months ago, he is now an expert. My people are of the Beta Israel in the Abyssinian highlands, a very ancient people. So, Negasi, we might be cousins!" Negasi smiled.

Beatriz pointed to a building ahead and asked, "Is that the Ahrida Synagogue?"

Negasi said, "I believe so. My friend suggested I ask the elders for help finding housing, and maybe work if we were so inclined."

The volunteers at the synagogue were very efficient. They had a list of housing possibilities. Alessandra asked, "Are Jews allowed to purchase rather than rent?"

"Yes, and I can tell you there are quite a few properties for sale in this district."

Ibrahim asked, "Are there any vacant apartment buildings for sale?"

"I think there are several, but they're fairly expensive because they're right on the water with boat docks."

Negasi looked at Ibrahim, who nodded. Then he looked at Alessandra, Afonso and Beatriz, who also nodded. Then he said, "We'd like to look at them. Can you give us the address and directions?"

"Certainly. They're not far."

The friends were overwhelmed when they finished looking at the three unoccupied properties. Afonso said, "The boat docks are quite large. They could accommodate two boats at least."

Ibrahim looked intrigued, but Negasi shook his head. "Like I said before, I think my piloting days are over."

Beatriz said, "I think I'll take up painting again. In the last few years running the inn, I wasn't able to do much painting. The views of the Golden Horn are gorgeous! And I love the beauty of the Arap Mosque. It looks pretty new."

Alessandra looked doubtful. "It looks like it might be a former church converted into a mosque. You should paint one of these grand mosques that seem to be everywhere."

As they walked up to the entrance to the Ahrida Synagogue, Alessandra said, "I can just feel my creative juices flowing again! I can finally whip my memoir into shape. Well, friends, it sounds like we're agreed. Which one shall we buy?"

Ibrahim's eyebrows shot up. "Just like that? No more looking at other properties?"

Negasi said, "Let's think about it for a day or two."

Twenty Years Later

Alessandra put down her memoir when she heard Ibrahim and Negasi laughing as they came in the front door. Her eyesight wasn't as good as it used to be but that was to be expected. *I just turned 80 years old; I suppose I should be thankful I've lived this long.* "What are you two lovers laughing about?"

Negasi said, "We just heard some very interesting news from Hikmet at the seaport. You remember how you used to stress that Grañ would come to power and try to conquer Abyssinia? Well, he just started his campaign. I wish our dear companion Afonso had lived long enough to hear this good news."

Alessandra said, "I miss him so much! This dear man's heart gave out. He used to complain of an irregular heartbeat. Finally, the irregularity lasted too long and his heart couldn't restore its rhythm."

Just then, Beatriz came in from her studio, where she had been painting. "What's all the noise? Can't a girl paint in peace around here?"

Alessandra said, "Shhh. Negasi is about to tell us about Grañ's quest for world domination. Or at least Abyssinian domination."

Negasi smiled. "Alessandra, it looks like your father's prediction is coming true about Grañ. First Harar, then… what?"

"As I recall my dad telling me, Grañ would begin his invasion of Abyssinia around 1529."

Ibrahim sat down at the dining table and laughed. "Well, we only have to wait another nine years. If we live long enough, we'll get to see him killed on the battlefield. When will that be… 1543?"

Beatriz laughed, "Dear God! We'll be 103. Who wants to live that long? Not me."

"I do. And so do you, cousin of mine. We have good genes, as my dad was fond of saying. I forget what genes are."

Beatriz said, "I remember how your dad explained them. They're little tiny things that live in your cells. They control things like our hair color, our eye color, our health, and so on. Little dictators, if you want to know the truth."

Negasi said, "Okay, Beatriz, we know you're impatient for us to ask you to show us your latest watercolor. So, please escort us into your salon."

Beatriz turned the easel around so it would face the room. "Voilà."

"I love it, dear Beatriz! Please, I do hope you're planning on framing it. I know just the person in the Covered Bazaar." Beatriz smiled, but didn't speak. Alessandra continued, "I see you identified the street where the artist is painting: '*Hazrat Selim.*' A lot of mosques were named after Sultan Selim. My personal favorite is the Selimiya up in Edirne."

When the friends were at dinner later that evening, Ibrahim asked Alessandra, "How are you doing with your memoir? Beatriz tells me you're just about finished."

"That's right. Actually, I finished it this morning. I'm pretty happy with it. It's too bad, though, that I can't show it to anyone other than my friends sitting at this table. I'm thinking of taking it to a printer to have it bound."

"Hmm," Beatriz said, "let me guess. You'll have it bound in black leather with chain stitching, and the word 'Gran' in Arabic and Amharic embossed on the cover. Am I right?"

"And why not? I know you like the idea; you're just pretending to be surprised."

Ibrahim grinned. "Will you be looking to have it read and critiqued by experienced literati?"

Alessandra smiled. "No, but I'll let you three read it. I'm warning you—I didn't leave anything out."

Negasi asked, "Once you've had it bound and embossed, what then? An archive or library somewhere?"

"I'm just going to keep it with me forever."

Negasi asked, "Forever? You're gonna take it to the grave with you?"

"And why not? I'll let you know if I change my mind."

"Why not find out where Vasco da Gama donated the astrolabe, assuming he did, and donate your book to keep it company?"

"Not with all the dangerous information in the book! Not as written, in English and Portuguese. Maybe if I could find an expert in some obscure language like... let me think... Tigrinya? A Semien Mountains cognate? Any ideas?"

Ibrahim and Negasi drummed their fingers on the dining table. Finally, Negasi looked at his partner and said, "How about you, Ibrahim?" Surely you know some obscure variant of Tigrinya that you could translate Alessandra's magnum opus into!"

"Hmm. I'll let you know when I find someone."

1545, Preparing for Eternity

Alessandra and Beatriz stood silently, leaning on their canes, in front of the graves of Ibrahim, Negasi and Afonso. Beatriz said, "Well, at least Negasi and Ibrahim got to hear the good news two years ago of Grañ's death on the battlefield. Negasi was very worried that Grañ might completely overrun Abyssinia."

"He needn't have worried. I told him many times that it was likely, at least in my father's history, that Grañ's campaign would come to an abrupt halt when he was killed on the battlefield. He died by the sword just as he caused so many others to die by the sword or worse."

Beatriz said, "At least they got to visit the land of Ibrahim's birth in Beta Israel. It was so sweet that Ibrahim offered to have your memoir placed in a synagogue library in his home village in the Semien Mountains."

Alessandra said, "I didn't take him up on the offer because I worried that eventually it would be found by someone. That would lead to untold mischief! I'm happy to have written it and shared it with my close friends, you and the guys. Somehow, I feel the memoir will have a home here with us." She placed a vase of roses on the grave holding their three friends. She brushed the dust off the headstone that stood between their friends' grave and the plot that would eventually hold the remains of Beatriz and Alessandra. Underneath the names "Afonso Escobar, Ibrahim Hasan and Negasi

Seyoum" carved into the marble was a blank space that would eventually say "Beatriz Lopes Nasi and Alessandra Mendes Fuente." In the space below their names was the inscription "Friends Forever."

The two cousins walked slowly back to their home on the waterfront. They were asking themselves the same question: *How much longer before we can join our friends?*

CHAPTER TWENTY-SIX

THE BOOK TRAVELS THROUGH TIME

Harrar, 1884

The wall around the Abyssinian city of Harar was in sad shape. In 1884, the French poet and traveler Arthur Rimbaud had established himself in the city as a merchant exporting coffee to Europe. He had befriended the governor, Ras Mekonnen, and convinced him to consider replacing part of the wall around the city. Inside one section of the wall was a very old library. "Your Excellency, I have spent hours in that library and, frankly, I am appalled at the conditions. I would recommend that the library be replaced by an export business."

"And I suppose that export business would be run by none other than the famous symbolist poet and libertine, Arthur Rimbaud. Am I right?"

Rimbaud smiled, trying to look modest and innocent at the same time. "Only if Your Excellency agrees, of course."

"And Your Excellency does agree. But the books must not be destroyed. I, too, have spent hours in the library and have found many ancient treatises that deserve a better home. So, I would have you organize an auction of the books, but an auction attended only by scholars and government representatives."

Rimbaud sent invitations to every academic, businessman and government official in the region. The auction took place on the date advertised. Many representatives of libraries, universities, madrasas and foreign consulates attended, including the 30-year-old Chinese consular officer, Yi Kang.

As he and the other prospective bidders toured the library, he was struck by one item in particular. It was a very old book, apparently hand-made. It had been wrapped in some kind of oilcloth. Rimbaud's assistant had opened up the oilcloth to allow the book itself to be seen. The book was bound in black leather. Embossed on the front cover were these strange words written in gold lettering—an Arabic word, عَرَانِي and an Amharic word ግራኝ.

Yi Kang's ability to read Arabic was minimal and his ability read Amharic was nonexistent. He mumbled to himself: "Even after studying Arabic for two years, I'm still pathetic." But he was able to pronounce the Arabic word by sounding out the letters. "'Grañ.' I have no idea what that means." As he held the book carefully, he felt an attraction to it. He was afraid to open the book at first for fear of damaging it. Even though his Confucian mind would disapprove of opening it, his Taoist inner training took over: *This book surely possesses some kind of powerful magic!* He held his breath, opened to the verso of the title page and saw that the book was written in 1455 in Mogadishu, Somalia.

Yi Kang was impressed with the way the book had been preserved inside the wall, not to mention the story of its age. He was convinced it was some sort of talisman. Accompanying the book was a handwritten memoir by Nur ibn Mujahid, who gave his title as the "Emir" of Harar. The auction note said that the memoir was written in colloquial Somaliña and was dated 1555.

Yi Kang was at the beginning of a long career as a representative of a group of Chinese trading families. He was posted to many cities over the next twenty years, always travelling with the book and memoir. He occasionally appended notes of his travels to the memoir.

Coming Home to Hawaii

Yi Kang retired in 1904 a wealthy man. He knew his meager salary from the Nanking government was not what made him wealthy. He was frugal and invested wisely. He was a 50-year-old widower with a 10-year-old son, Yong Shen. They settled in Honolulu and lived there for twenty years. When he heard about a 16-room mansion outside the village of Kaunakakai on Molokai, he immediately purchased it. He was 70.

Although Yi Kang had continued adding to the memoir throughout those years, he was concerned about his "addiction" to having the book and memoir always with him in his travels. He believed he was becoming somewhat eccentric. The indigenous inhabitants of Kaunakakai certainly thought so and generally shunned him. Suspecting the book was the cause of his eccentricity, he placed the book and memoir at the bottom of a trunk filled with old clothes and books. He put the trunk inside a crate and stored it in one of the attics.

Lost and Found

Yi Kang lived in Kaunakakai for 20 more years and died in 1944 at the age of 90. In his will he bequeathed the mansion "and all its contents" to his 50-year-old son. Yong Shen, who never explored the extremely cluttered attic, willed the mansion to his 40-year-old son Hak Hoi Liu 20 years later in 1964. Liu, living in Honolulu, refused to live in the mansion, believing it haunted. He died intestate at age 90 in 2014.

Liu's daughter took possession of the mansion and lived there with her 40-year-old son, Mon Lao, for only one year before dying of cancer in 2015 at the age of 73.

Mon Lao was more than a little eccentric, but most of that was due to his extreme condition of ADD. He never married and was illiterate. After 2 years he had spent the majority of the money in his mother's estate. He opened up the attics and emptied them in search of anything of value that he could sell. In two of the attics he found expensive antiques and rugs. In another attic he found a crate containing the trunk and assorted junk. He opened the trunk and saw it was filled with books, papers and old clothes. He didn't bother to empty it and left it in the attic with the other junk.

In 2017 Mon Lao became too ill to take care of the house, so he put it up for sale. He reviewed at least a dozen offers before one just jumped out at him—from João da Gama. Mon Lao was intrigued by the man's name; he vaguely recalled from his school days the name Vasco da Gama, a maritime explorer. He also was inclined to sell to da Gama based on the fact that he was a retired history professor. He decided on the spot to accept da Gama's offer and was out of there in less than a month. He died six months later.

CHAPTER TWENTY-SEVEN

BACK TO THE FUTURE

A Surprise in the Attic

João da Gama had been too busy preparing for his upcoming retirement to explore the derelict mansion in Kaunakakai he had just purchased. It had 16 rooms and half a dozen attics. In João's career he had explored archives, outbuildings and attics hunting for primary documents related to various research projects. He knew he would explore the mansion's attics before doing anything else. But in 2018, a year after the purchase, João finally began repairing the mansion and emptying the attics. Unlike Mon Lao, the strange little guy who sold him the mansion, João's curiosity was piqued when he found the trunk full of books and clothes.

João had been a history professor specializing in early contacts between Africa and China. He was astounded when he found what looked to be an extremely ancient book under the clothes. The leather-bound book was written longhand in modern English and the sections were sewn together. The inscription on the verso gave the date as 1455 and the location as Mogadishu, Somalia. Accompanying the book was a handwritten memoir written in Chinese.

João took the book and memoir downstairs to give them his close attention. He was amused to find that a man named Horacio Fuente wrote the book. Despite the late hour, he decided to give his own Horacio Fuente a call. "Listen, my friend. You're famous!"

"Well, I already knew that. What else is new? But wait… why are you just now telling me this? Haven't you been following the meteoric rise of my career?"

"Sure. I have. We all have. But listen, I'm telling you this because I want you to meet me tomorrow morning, 10 a.m., at the Starbucks next to the Molokai Hilton. I figure the prospect of a mystery revealed would get you to come."

"Why in the fuck did you call me at 11 p.m. just to lure me into some kind of intrigue? I'm an old man. Hell, you're an old man, too! But I'll play your game. Can I bring my wife? She loves mysteries."

"Certainly. I was just going to say that. Bring Mariana along. Unless you're worried about her advanced state of pregnancy."

"She's a trooper, as we both know. Those Somali women… they can take anything."

The next morning, Horacio and Mariana walked into the cafe fashionably late. João put down his coffee and said, "What took you so long? I've been sitting at this table for half an hour."

"Liar. You probably just got here yourself. I can see your plate of sunny-side-up eggs hasn't been touched." Horacio pulled out a chair and offered it to Mariana. Then he noticed that his friend was wearing a pair of those thin gloves your hygienist wears when he or she cleans your teeth.

João said, "You look mighty pregnant, young woman. How many months?"

"My doc says I've got another month to endure this torture. I'm telling you—I feel so ready to deliver this child! And I'm hungry all the time." João was distracted by what Horacio was saying, and ignored Mariana's hint.

Horacio said, "We think we've agreed on a name, or I should say, we've narrowed it down to two."

"So, what are they?"

"Not so fast. You demanded an audience to this big mystery you woke me up to tell me about. So, first things first. Out with it. And tell me why you're wearing gloves."

"You'll see why in a minute." João reached into his backpack sitting on the floor and pulled out a Tupperware container. He opened it and took out a book and a manila folder. The book was wrapped in black oilcloth. He set both on the table. Horacio reached for the book but João stopped him. "Not so fast. We must be careful. This baby is 563 years old, published in 1455." He reached into his backpack, took out a box of Nitrile gloves, handed a pair to Horacio and told him to put them on.

Mariana asked, "What's in the folder? Is that a 500-year-old manila folder?"

"Very funny. But some of the papers inside might be 200 years old; pure linen. Other papers are much older. It looks like there are two memoirs, one in Somaliña written in Arabic script, and one in Chinese. The handwriting is almost illegible. I can't read either language anyway. I'll show the Chinese one to Yuen Monday. I thought Mariana might want to take a crack at the Somaliña memoir." He gave her a pair of gloves to her, took the loose pages out of the folder and handed them to her.

She looked through the pages and set them down. "The handwriting is terrible and faint. I'd go blind trying to read this." She stared at the book. "One of the words embossed on the cover—ግራኝ— is `Grañ' in Amharic. The same word in Arabic, عراني, is below that. I have no idea what the word means. I don't know much Amharic. The word doesn't mean anything in Arabic or Somaliña."

Horacio said, "Okay. Let's get to the book. What's the title?"

João turned the book around and opened it so Horacio and Mariana could read the title page. After a few seconds, Mariana laughed and said, "You are famous, dear. João's right."

Horacio read the title aloud: "From Portugal to Mogadishu, by Horacio Fuente, retired notary and scribe." Horacio said, "The title's in English. I didn't know English was spoken in Mogadishu. And why would the Portuguese author write a book in English? Do you mind if I take a look at the binding, etc.? After all, I've handled quite a few rare and ancient books in my day."

As Horacio carefully turned the pages, João turned to his neglected, lukewarm breakfast. Mariana said, "Since my husband is so engrossed in his masterpiece, might I have a few bites of your eggs. I didn't have breakfast." João smiled, placed half of his eggs on the toast plate and pushed the plate over to Mariana.

Horacio finally looked up. "This is so amazing. This Horacio Fuente was born in Portugal and emigrated to North Africa and then Somalia. Quite a career he had there, I must say."

Mariana put down her fork and said, "Somalia? What about Somalia? How could a Portuguese man ever have lived in Somalia in… what year? 15th century? He would have been killed!"

João took the book back and opened it up to a drawing of a spherical astrolabe. "Now check out this baby:

"The author describes how he found the device. And how his daughter met the famous explorer, my illustrious ancestor I might add, Vasco da Gama, and gave the Great Navigator the device. And another astonishing thing is the language itself—he wrote the book in English; not archaic English, modern English!" João smiled and added, "And I've saved the best for last. I don't know if you noticed, Horacio, but the author's daughter and niece are… wait. Tell me again what you've decided to name your daughter."

"Wow, that's quite a change of subject, Mr. da Gama." Mariana smiled and looked at her husband. "Now, Horacio, have you been spreading rumors about our daughter?"

"What rumors? You never said I couldn't tell anyone."

João said, "Oh come on, you two. Out with it—what names are you considering?"

"Well, I favor Alessandra, and Mariana favors Beatriz."

João opened the book to the middle and read out loud: "Mariana and I were so proud at the news that our beloved daughter Alessandra was accepted as the first female student at the University of Padua. Even her cousin Beatriz was proud. There was not a hint of jealousy."

Mariana and Horacio were speechless. Then they broke out laughing. Horacio said, "Well, dear, it looks like whichever name we choose, our daughter has already gone down in history."

Mariana said, "And we've gone down in history, too. But before we go on, I just want to point out another historical oddity. The author says his daughter will be the first female accepted into the University of Padua. But as you know, João, no European university admitted female students until well into the 17th century. So, my question is, where in the hell did this book come from?" Chuckling, she said, "Maybe an alternate history? A parallel history?"

"Please, Mariana, control yourself." Horacio ducked just before his wife could clobber him with her napkin.

João said, "Well, the first thing I'm gonna do Monday is take this book into the forensics lab at U of H and ask them to run a test on the book's paper. Maybe this is an elaborate forgery."

Horacio looked up from the drawing of the spherical astrolabe and said, "And while you're at it, ask our colleagues in the history department if they've ever put their hands on a device like that." He turned the page and said, "Not only that, but it says on the page after that illustration that the author got hold of this device from a shipwreck off of Mozambique. Mozambique is quite far south of

Mogadishu. It would be great to find out whether Vasco da Gama actually had it and if so, what he did with it."

"Yes, my ancestor, no doubt! I wonder if that actually happened. Or maybe it only happened in the author's world, the mythical world of Horacio Fuente."

Mariana ate the last bite of João's toast and said, "One way to find out, my friend. Go online and see if there are any museums with artifacts from Vasco da Gama! I'd bet dollars to donuts Portugal has one."

"That's a great idea! And that leads me to my next revelation. I haven't told you yet, but I just heard that my grant application was approved. I'll be visiting sites of former Sephardic Jewish communities in Portugal, Spain and Turkey. Maybe I'll look for archives of Vasco da Gama's writings and artifacts while I'm in Portugal. You guys wanna join me?"

Horacio looked up from the book and said, "We aren't going anywhere for at least a couple of years, until our daughter is old enough to travel." Turning to Mariana he said, "Hey, when she's old enough, let's go to Mogadishu and see if the inn that our namesakes owned is still there. The book describes this huge, two-story place in the shape of a `U' with a garden in the middle. I'd be up for it."

"Well, my dear Horacio, it'll be a cold day in hell before I set foot in Somalia again. Send me a post card, one with a nice photo of bombed-out Mogadishu. I'll read it to our daughter, Alessandra Beatriz Fuente."

ABOUT THE AUTHOR

After 23 years practicing law with the California Attorney General's Office in San Francisco, and teaching for 13 semesters in Golden Gate's Appellate Advocacy program part time as an adjunct professor, I retired in 2011 and began writing fiction and memoirs. My first opus was a novella, *My Brother's Keeper*, loosely based on the circumstances of my younger brother's murder. Next came a novel, *Stolen Identity*, published in 2015, and its sequel, *Unfinished Business*, in 2017. *Trial and Error*, the third novel in the trilogy that began with *Stolen Identity* came out in 2021. My novel *The Mystic and the Warrior* came out in 2021.

The novel you are holding in your hands is a composite of two previously self-published novels—*The Spherical Astrolabe* and *Around the Horn and Back*.

My short story *One More Race Before We Die* was published in 2019 in the University of Hawaii eZine, Vice-Versa. I included that story in my *Collected Stories* in 2021.

I published three memoirs in 2021: *A Pirate Forever, From Librarian to Lawyer, Life as a Peace Corps Volunteer, Ethiopia and Eritrea, 1972-74*, and *The Happy Wanderer*. While still a law student at Golden Gate, I served on the Law Review and published an article, *"Qualified Immunity for INS Church-Busters? Presbyterian Church (U.S.A.) v. United States*, Golden Gate University Law Review, Ninth Circuit Survey, Volume 20, Number 1, Spring 1990. In the year 2000 I published a memoir of my Peace Corps experience in Asmara, Eritrea, in the Peace Corps Writers anthology, *Eritrea Remembered: Recollections and Photos by Peace Corps Volunteers*.

SELECTED WORK by MICHAEL BANISTER
(in chronological order)

My Brother's Keeper

A drug courier crashes his plane in a frozen lake in Yosemite's high country. Winston, a Yosemite "valley rat" on the run from killers in his home town, discovers the plane during a winter hike. He off loads the cargo and begins a new life as a drug dealer. After he and his girlfriend are murdered during a drug deal gone south, their two unrelated children, Josh and Kathy, are raised by their respective grandparents. When Josh asks his Uncle Mark for help in finding his "sister," the outcome is anything but predictable.

Stolen Identity

Dushan's dreams had always been unusual—sometimes scary, sometimes exhilarating. But ever since he was seven years old his dreams took on another dimension—it was like he was awake inside them. His mother—who he thought had been killed in the Yugoslavian civil war when he was a baby—was talking to him, telling him she was alive and living with his father—who was supposed to have been lost at sea during a fishing expedition in the North Sea. In each of those dreams, Dushan was unable to respond and tell his parents that he was living with his "adopted" family in California and was best friends with his "stepbrother" Danilo. The two stepbrothers were now teenagers and occasionally popped up in one another's dreams, sharing their impressions after waking up.

However, the time for dreaming was past—they were about to embark on a desperate attempt to escape their abusive father, the man who arranged to steal Dushan from his real father and plant the lie that his real parents were dead. Their attempt succeeded on one level, but the consequences were completely unexpected.

Unfinished Business

The exciting sequel to "Stolen Identity," the story of a stolen boy and his beloved "stepbrother" growing into manhood and bringing their two families together. Now, they discover they have some unfinished business to take care of and some very unpleasant people to deal with. This gripping tale follows these young men and their families through Britain, Ireland and Slovenia as they attempt to put an end to the tragedies that brought them all together in the first place.

Trial and Error

Dushan Sava was in trouble. Accused of stealing the identity of the victim of a horrific traffic accident, and then impersonating him as a college student, Dushan, an illegal immigrant, had to flee the country using the victim's passport. A year later, after having obtained his own passport and returned to the US, he accompanied a friend who would soon join the faculty at Rutgers University. Dushan's former roommate saw him on campus, and Dushan was arrested and put on trial. The outcome of the trial was anything but certain.

The Mystic and the Warrior

Who was the man who called himself Shamsuddin? In post-war Valletta, on the island of Malta, he lived in a part of the city that still hadn't recovered from the destruction of World War Two. In 1955, Shamsuddin lived in a bombed-out post office and sold antiques and other valuable items. When a group of five young men from Istanbul paid a visit looking for such things they had heard Shamsuddin could sell them, the parting gifts he provided them were much more than gifts—the young men soon discovered they couldn't bear to be without them.

Forty years later, Shamsuddin's business had radically changed. He had allied himself with Turgut Evren, a Colonel in the Turkish military. Each man had a hidden agenda—hidden from society and hidden from each other. And the five men who were no longer young? What was their destiny in this evolving story?

Life as a Peace Corps Volunteer Ethiopia and Eritrea, 1972-74
A collection of aerogrammes, memoirs and photos from my two years as a Peace Corps Volunteer in Ethiopia and Eritrea, 1972-74.

A Pirate Forever!
A memoir of my life growing up in Japan, Austria, Germany and California.

The Happy Wanderer
A collection of memoirs of my travel and work, 1974-2021, in Seattle, Tunisia, Berkeley, Turkey, Oakland and Ireland.

Collected Stories

Four stories:

One More Race Before We Die—Three race car drivers killed in a race ask a Las Vegas magician to stage a race to allow the dead drivers to finish the race.

Gino di Lampedusa—A genie on the lam from an evil genie in his own world passes through the veil and asks a Las Vegas magician to help him capture and neutralize the evil genie.

Whitethorn, 1969—a backwoods commune terrorizes a group of back-to-the-land hippies.

My Brother's Keeper—a loosely based story based on the murder of the author's drug-dealing brother.

9 781950 562534